THE MONSTER FACTORY

Richard Rainey

A WORDSMITH BOOK

New York

Maxwell Macmillan Canada
Toronto

Maxwell Macmillan International
New York   Oxford   Singapore   Sydney

Book design and production: Deborah Fillion
Cover design and artwork: Ted Bernstein
Photographs of Doyle, Irving, Shelley, and Wells: The Bettmann Archive
Photographs of Leroux, Stevenson, and Stoker: The Granger Collection

New Discovery Books
Macmillan Publishing Company
866 Third Avenue
New York, NY 10022

Maxwell Macmillan Canada, Inc.
1200 Eglinton Avenue East
Suite 200
Don Mills, Ontario M3C 3N1

Macmillan Publishing Company is part of the Maxwell Communication
Group of Companies.

First edition
Printed in the United States of America

10 9 8 7 6 5 4 3 2 1

Library of Congress Cataloging-in-Publication Data

Rainey, Richard.
    The monster factory / Richard Rainey.
        p.   cm.
    "A Wordsmith Book."
    Includes bibliographical references.
    Summary: Discusses the lives and works of the creators of famous
monster literature: Mary Shelley, Bram Stoker, Washington Irving, H.G.
Wells, Arthur Conan Doyle, Robert Louis Stevenson, and Gaston Leroux.
    ISBN 0-02-775663-7
    1. Horror tales—History and criticism—Juvenile literature.
2. Monsters in literature—Juvenile literature.   3. Authors—Biography—
Juvenile literature. [1. Authors.   2. Monsters in literature.   3. Horror
stories—History and criticism.]   I. Title.
PN3433.8.R36   1993
809.3'8738—dc20   92-26191

This book is dedicated to:
my mother, Joan Rainey, who opened
up the world of books for me and so
many others; my wife and research
assistant, Mary; and of course, my
daughter, Susan, and my son, Charles,
for saying, "Why don't you write
something we'd like to read?"

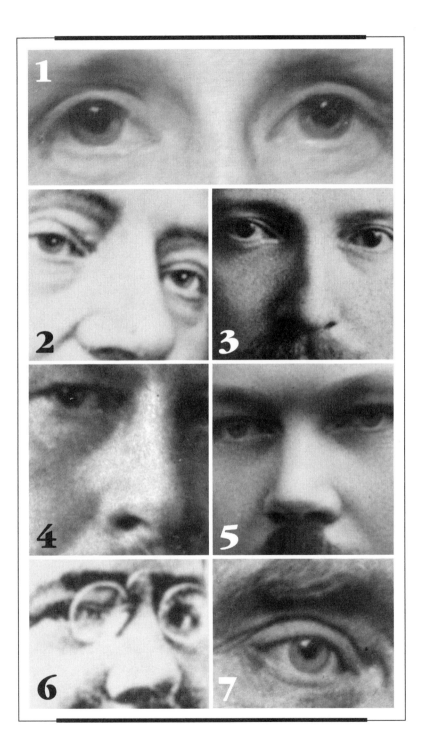

Contents

Introduction

Monsters have lurked in the shadows of the human mind from the beginning of time, and ever since then we have been trying to capture them. From crude pictures painted on cave walls to stories told around the safety of a fire, people have searched the darkest corners of their imaginations to confront the things that terrify them the most.

Nowhere is this more apparent than in storytelling. A long, long time ago, people used stories about thunder gods and river goddesses to explain lightning and floods. In Russia, whenever a forest shook during a storm, it was said that the Leshye, great furry green forest dwellers, were wrestling. If a sailor became dazzled by the ocean waves and jumped overboard, the Welsh said it was because he heard the voice of a mermaid calling him into the waves.

Shelley

Over the years the style of storytelling changed, and so did the forms the monsters took. The earliest monsters to haunt the pages of literature were quite literally monsters—animals of "strange and terrifying shape"—as defined by the dictionary.

One of the first such monsters to crawl out of the shadows and onto the page was Grendel, the hideous marsh creature who prowls through the epic poem *Beowulf,* written in the seventh or

Irving

Stevenson

eighth century. The author of *Beowulf* is unknown, but whoever wrote it created a beast that has terrified readers for centuries.

Grendel is the perfect monster. With his mouth filled with razor-sharp teeth and his limb-shredding claws, this ogre creeps into a Danish castle and kills 30 knights at one sitting. After tearing them limb from limb and drinking their blood, he drags their lifeless corpses back to his lair.

Then enters Beowulf, a fearless Swedish warrior who arrives at the castle with a shipload of brave knights. Wise in the ways of dragon slaying and monster mashing, this Viking chieftain takes on Grendel in a wrestling match beneath the waves. After a fight in which Beowulf also destroys Grendel's mother, an even more terrifying mon-ster than her son, peace is restored to the castle.

Stoker

Most likely, Grendel had his true beginnings as one of the wild creatures that lived on the moors and occasionally attacked wandering humans, much like the werewolves of English legend. As the centuries passed and creatures of the wild became less of a threat to civilized people, new kinds of monsters appeared on the horizon. These monsters lived much closer to home and looked more and more like the people they preyed upon.

Doyle

In the 14th century, another epic poem sur-faced, this one also written by an unknown hand. In *Sir Gawain and the Green Knight,* the knights of King Arthur's round table are just sitting down to a New Year's feast when a monstrous green figure rides his equally green war-horse into their hall.

The Green Knight issues a challenge to the knights. If anyone among them is brave enough to strike his neck with the great green-and-gold ax he carries and kills him, he will be rewarded. But if he lives, the Green Knight will return the blow one year later.

Leroux

When only King Arthur himself dares to accept the challenge, Sir Gawain steps in and takes his place. He grabs the ax and swings its four-foot blade at the Green Knight. The green head drops to the floor. A moment later, the Green Knight calmly picks up his head and rides from the hall. As he leaves, his severed head reminds Gawain of their bargain, telling him to come to the Green Chapel in the woods one year later to fulfill the bargain.

A year to the day later, Sir Gawain arrives at the Green Chapel to face the Knight. The Green Knight swings his ax, but only nicks the knight's neck. He releases Sir Gawain, telling him that his bravery has proven his worthiness to be a knight.

The Green Knight introduced a new kind of monster, one that was not much different from the other people in the story or

Wells

from the people reading the story. These are perhaps the most terrifying monsters of all, the kind who can live among us undetected until the moment they reveal themselves as the creatures of darkness that they really are.

These are the kinds of monsters we are out to capture in the pages of this book. Dracula, the Frankenstein monster, the Headless Horseman, the Phantom of the Opera, Dr. Jekyll and Mr. Hyde, the Hound of the Baskervilles—their names strike terror into the hearts of readers everywhere. Just as their forerunners made people bar the castle doors a little more securely or put another log on the fire to make it burn more brightly, these denizens of the imagination awaken fears we thought we had conquered. They make us check under our beds and jump at shadows, afraid of what may be lurking around the corner.

But unlike Grendel and the Green Knight, we know the origins of these monsters. We know who created them and can follow the events in the lives of the authors who brought these monsters to life between the covers of books. We can see the very real people and happenings that became transformed into the nightmare worlds of Bram Stoker's *Dracula,* H. G. Wells's *The Invisible Man,* Mary Shelley's *Frankenstein,* and other favorites.

The following chapters will take you into the pages of some of the most terrifying pieces of literature ever written and into the lives of the people who wrote them. You will see how these writers looked deep into themselves and discovered dark and fearsome monsters—monsters still haunting us long after they first stalked across the fictional landscapes of their creators' imaginations.

Don't forget to bring a flashlight.

Chapter 1

Frankenstein's Folly

The Ice-Bound Soul

A huge shape comes out of the frozen mist, pulled across the Arctic ice by a dogsled team.

From half a mile away, sailors aboard a ship surrounded by creeping and creaking ice swarm to the deck to study this strange sight. Strange because they are in the middle of nowhere, stranded in a barren white landscape where no human can survive.

But the shape is not human.

He is both something more and something less. He is a "monster" created by a man. With inhuman strength and a rapidly growing intelligence, the monster is able to survive in this cold wasteland where no human can. But sadly, he cannot survive in civilization. Men and women find him too horrible to look at, too different to welcome to their homes and hearths.

The day after the sailors first see the monster, they see another shape moving across the ice behind a dogsled. This shape is definitely a man—the half-frozen, half-crazed scientist Victor Frankenstein, who is determined to follow his monstrous creation to the ends of the earth and destroy him. But too weak to continue the hunt, Frankenstein is brought aboard the ice-bound ship by Captain Robert Walton, who listens to his story and then narrates to us the long and sad history of the nameless monster.

* * *

So begins Mary Shelley's novel *Frankenstein.* By the time the story ends, the reader is left wondering who was the real monster—the manmade creature or the man who made him? Still other questions come to mind after reading *Frankenstein.* What was the person like who wrote it? And how in the world did she write such a great novel at the age of 19?

Castles in the Air

Mary Shelley grew up in a house full of books, a London bookshop at 41 Skinner Street, where pages endlessly turned and rustled like leaves in an enchanted forest.

Her father, William Godwin, was a bookseller and occasional publisher who wrote books on history and politics, as well as a supernatural novel or two.

Many famous writers of the time often visited the shop to talk about their work, their lives, and their hopes and politics. And Mary Shelley listened eagerly, sometimes taking part in the spirited conversations. While other young children often studied about writers in books, she had a chance to observe them firsthand. In such an atmosphere, it was only natural that she would become a writer.

Her mother, Mary Wollstonecraft Godwin, was also a writer. A free spirit who was about 200 years ahead of her time, she published revolutionary novels and books, such as *A Vindication of the Rights of Woman.* Unfortunately, Mary's mother died 11 days after giving birth to her in 1797. William Godwin remarried, and although her stepmother was kind to her, Mary often thought

Mary Wollstonecraft Shelley

about her real mother and missed her a great deal. Fortunately, she still had a chance to get to know her through the books her mother wrote and the memories her father shared with her.

Mary and her sisters were schooled at home by her father and stepmother in arts and languages. Even as young children they wrote stories and novels and spun elaborate fantasies. As Mary wrote in an introduction to a special edition of *Frankenstein* that was issued 15 years after the book's first publication, she spent most of her free time as a child writing stories or building "castles in the air—the indulging in waking dreams—the following up trains of thought.... My dreams were at once more fantastic and agreeable than my writings."

Soon her dreams and writings would come together and lead to the creation of the novel—and the creature—that nearly everyone in the modern world has heard of.

In such a literary atmosphere it was also only natural that Mary would fall in love with a man who could have stepped from the pages of a Victorian romance novel. He was handsome, walked with a limp, and came from a noble family. But he was considered something of a rebel by British high society because of his scandalous essays and poems. His name was Percy Bysshe Shelley, and his fame had preceded him to the bookshop on Skinner Street long before he first walked through the door and met young Mary.

Soon after the two of them met, their lives became a real-life romance, full of wonder and sorrow and tragedy. Though she was only 16, and Shelley was married, Mary ran off with him and traveled through Europe. That tour of countrysides, castles, and cold forbidding mountains was the subject of her first book,

A Six Weeks' Tour. And though many literary magazines reviewed the book favorably, it was nothing like the things to come. For her greatest book would come from travels to a much stranger and distant land—the land of her imagination.

On several extended stays with relatives in Scotland as a young girl, Mary had walked along the cold seashore, soaking up the desolate atmosphere and conjuring up strange stories. Perhaps it was there in Scotland, while she looked toward the faraway Arctic Ocean, that she first saw a sea captain named Robert Walton who would tell the story of Frankenstein to the world.

Mary was just 19 when she began work on the book that would place her and her creation on the literary map. The story of how she came to write *Frankenstein* is almost as strange as the story itself.

The Haunted Shores

The haunting began in Switzerland on the night of June 16, 1816, while a cold summer rain swept in from Lake Geneva and drummed like spectral hoofbeats on the rooftop of Villa Diodati. That was the night Mary Shelley began to dream a dream that would be shared by millions of readers when her book *Frankenstein, or The Modern Prometheus* was published. It was also a dream that in many ways would come horribly true for her. For the losses she suffered during her lifetime paralleled many of the things she wrote in that tragic and most haunting novel.

Mary and Percy Shelley were gathered around a roaring fireplace with Mary's half sister Claire, the famous poet Lord Byron, and Byron's doctor, John Polidori. They were taking turns reading ghost stories out loud, filling the ember-scorched air with tales of haunted castles, floating skulls, and wedding-gowned ghosts.

After they read a number of stories, it was Byron who suddenly suggested that each of them write an original ghost story. The challenge was accepted by all of them, and they proceeded to create eerie tales to read to one another.

Unlike the others, who rapidly developed stories, Mary couldn't come up with an idea that she was happy with. She tried, she later wrote, to create a story that would "make the reader dread to look round, to curdle the blood, and quicken the beatings of the heart." Mary spent much of her waking time worrying about it, with little success. But fortunately, she spent much of her sleeping time weaving the tale.

While Mary had to struggle with her idea, Byron immediately came up with a story about a vampire who traveled across Europe in high society and drained the lifeblood of his acquaintances. John Polidori was so taken with Byron's idea that he embellished it a good deal and began working on what would become the first popular vampire novel when it was published years later under the title *The Vampyre*.

Ironically, publication of that book also birthed an enduring legend about a ghostwriter. When *The Vampyre* first appeared, the author's name was printed as Lord Byron. Later, when the book became successful, it appeared in print with the byline John Polidori. Ever since then, book critics have argued about who really wrote the book. Some critics think that Byron wrote the book and later allowed Polidori to put his name to it. Other critics insist that Polidori wrote it and originally used Byron's more

famous name on the byline so that it would have a better chance of being popular with the public.

Though *The Vampyre* and its evil main character, Lord Ruthven, was well known in its time, Polidori's story is pretty much forgotten today, while Mary Shelley's *Frankenstein* is known throughout the world.

So of the two monster novels that were born that strange night in 1816, Polidori's went the way of the ghost, dimly remembered and rarely seen, while Mary Shelley's monster began a growth spurt still going on to this day.

The monster came at night.

Mary was lying in her bed thinking about the unusual conversation Percy and Byron had been engaged in all day. The two poets were discussing the latest scientific advances of the time. Most exciting to them was the experiment of Dr. Erasmus Darwin (Charles Darwin's grandfather), who preserved a piece of vermicelli under glass until "by some extraordinary means it began to move with voluntary motion." If a scientist could make a piece of nonliving matter come to life, Mary thought, how much easier it should be to make a dead body come back to life.

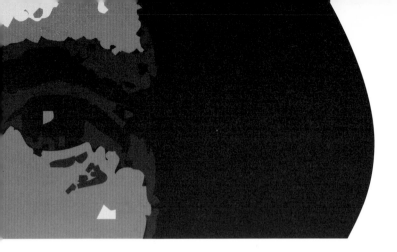

As Mary wrote about the intriguing conversation, "Perhaps the component parts of a creature might be manufactured, brought together, and endued with vital warmth." In other words, take several parts from dead human bodies, add a jolt of electricity, and a monster is born.

The haunting idea would not go away. As she lay down on her bed she couldn't sleep. Nor could she think about anything else. All she could do was watch this vision unfold before her. "I saw—with shut eyes, but acute mental vision—I saw the pale student of unhallowed arts kneeling beside the thing he had put together. I saw the hideous phantasm of a man stretched out, and then, on the working of some powerful engine, show signs of life, and stir with an uneasy, half-vital motion."

The vision continued until finally she saw a scientist restlessly sleeping in his bed only to be awakened by the huge monster he'd created in his laboratory, this horrible-looking creature he'd given life to, staring down at him.

Mary's eyes snapped open, terrified by the secret sights she'd seen. The fear and the thrill of the vision held a grip on her. "I could not so easily get rid of my hideous phantom; still it haunted me." In the morning, she began writing the story.

When she showed it to her husband, Percy Shelley thought it

was such a unique idea that he encouraged her to turn it into a novel instead of just a short story.

Monster at Large

The first time we see Mary Shelley's monster he is literally heading for the end of the earth to lose himself in the cold and barren wasteland. He's a terrifying sight. But it didn't have to be this way. The monster could have been a loving creature, a help to humanity rather than a curse.

But the man who created him, the young and brilliant scientist Victor Frankenstein, gave little thought to the tremendous amount of care such a creature would need. He was more interested in the challenge of blending ancient alchemy with modern science to restore life to a patchwork creature of scattered limbs, organs, and eyes. By studying old books on magic along with the new magic of mathematics and electricity, he finally discovered the secret of life itself.

And then he bestowed this gift upon the corpse in his dark laboratory. Early in the novel, Victor Frankenstein narrates how this miraculous event came about.

> *It was on a dreary night of November, that I beheld the accomplishment of my toils. With an anxiety that almost amounted to agony, I collected the instruments of life around me, that I might infuse a spark of being into the lifeless thing that lay at my feet. It was already one in the morning;*

the rain pattered dismally against the panes, and my candle was nearly burnt out, when, by the glimmer of the half-extinguished light, I saw the dull yellow eye of the creature open, it breathed hard, and a convulsive motion agitated its limbs.

Now that the creature was alive, the scientist saw him in a different light. He was not the beautiful angel of Frankenstein's dreams, but a huge misshapen thing with yellow skin and watery eyes and cold black lips.

Victor Frankenstein hurried from the laboratory, leaving his creation to fend for itself on the operating table. And then he fell into a restless sleep full of nightmares.

The nightmare continued when he awoke. For standing by his bed was the huge monster, trying to talk to his creator, making animal-like sounds, opening his jaws, and fixing his eyes on the scientist who'd tried to escape him in sleep. It was as if the creature were saying, "You created me, now care for me. Help me."

But Victor Frankenstein cared only for himself. In fear and disgust he ran from his room, ran from the "magical" creature he'd given life to, and abandoned him to his own fate.

Left on his own, the monster wandered out into a cold and unfriendly world. In a later section of the novel that is narrated by the monster himself, we learn what happened to him next.

Roaming the mountainous countryside, hungry and uncertain of what to do, he finds food in a peasant's hut. Unintentionally, he scares the peasant away. Next he encounters a group of villagers who scream at the sight of him. They throw rocks and chase after him as if he is a wild dog.

Alone, not understanding why people hate him, the monster hides in a small hovel next to a cottage and watches the people inside. He begins to get used to their routine, secretly helping them stock supplies of wood for the fire. He almost starts to think of them as his family. For the first time he is part of a human community, even though they aren't aware of him.

He studies them to learn about humanity. Through the chilling winter he listens to them as they read aloud from books, and this gives him the education about the world that he sought. One thing puzzles him, though. According to the books, men and women are noble, kind, and courageous beings. But if that's true, he wonders, why are they all so vicious to him?

The creature continues his education by eavesdropping on the conversations in the cottage, a hidden student of humanity. One day he finds some books dropped outside the cottage and slowly learns to read. Then he finds some papers in the clothes he took from Victor Frankenstein's room when he fled. Now that he can read, he sees that the papers are an account of how he came to be created by the scientist. And he feels hatred for the man who created him and abandoned him, left him alone and friendless in a world created and ruled by humans.

Finally, when only the old man who lives with his grown children is in the house, the monster pays him a visit. Because the old man is blind, he is the first one who really *sees* the monster for what he is—a fellow creature in need of friendship. He finds the creature to be a pleasant sort and, simply by talking with him as an equal, gives him the first genuine bit of human companionship he has had in his short life.

But then the rest of the family returns. Instead of a creature craving love and affection, they see a hulking monster in their cottage and they attack him. Though he could easily defeat them, the great creature runs away. The blows from their sticks don't hurt him. Rather, it is a deeper hurt he takes with him, the hurt of a lonely being who feels the loss of human kindness.

It is at this point that the monster becomes a truly dangerous creation. He travels back to Victor Frankenstein's college to confront his creator, revealing to him that he's the one who killed Frankenstein's younger brother. He forces Frankenstein to agree to create another being, a female this time, so that the creature can have the companionship of someone like him.

Frankenstein agrees. At first. But then he betrays the creature once more and destroys the female creature he was about to give life to. So the monster is truly alone, forever doomed to wander the earth without love and hope. And so he decides to bestow that same fate upon his creator.

He kills Victor Frankenstein's best friend.

Then he kills Frankenstein's new bride.

And finally it is clear to Frankenstein once and for all that the only thing he can really be wedded to is a quest to destroy the great creature itself—married in a vow of mutual hatred. He sets off on his voyage, pursuing the monster across Europe and picking up clues that he has been seen passing before him. The trail leads north, until finally Frankenstein closes in on the strange monstrous shape sledding across the Arctic ice.

But by this time the creator is too weak to go on. Only his creature can survive in the brutal climate of the unforgiving north. Taken aboard the ship in a state of collapse, Victor Frankenstein tells his tale to the explorer Robert Walton, who in turn recounts the narratives of the scientist and the monster in a number of letters to his sister at home in England, far away from this desolate world.

At the novel's end the scientist lies dead on board the ship . . . and the monster comes to look upon the man who created him.

Now that the scientist is dead, the monster's thirst for vengeance is also dead.

Finally free of all the bonds he had with humanity, the monster leaves the ship, determined to destroy himself—and perhaps meet his maker in the next world. "My ashes will be swept into the sea by the winds," says the creature. "My spirit will sleep in peace; or if it thinks, it will not surely think thus. Farewell." The monster has assumed full control of his destiny at last.

We see him one more time through the captain's eyes. "He sprung from the cabin-window, as he said this, upon the ice-raft which lay close to the vessel. He was soon borne away by the waves, and lost in darkness and distance."

Weird Science

Mary Shelley's novel presents Victor Frankenstein to us as a brilliant scientist, a man far ahead of his time. After all, Frankenstein discovered the secret of life. He found a way to reanimate a corpse through some strange process that had eluded the greatest minds for centuries.

At least, we are told he found that great secret. But nowhere in the book is it explained what that secret is. As Frankenstein tells the captain of the ship who rescued him, it is such a great and terrible secret that he doesn't want to reveal it to anyone else.

In the 1800s science was entering a new stage where anything seemed possible. In the preface to her novel, Shelley even wrote that some scientists of the time thought that the things she wrote about really could happen. Who knew what strange powers lurked in the shadows of science?

After all, the scientists in Mary Shelley's time were announcing new discoveries all the time. From 1800 to the time she wrote her book a number of amazing scientific discoveries were made.

Infrared solar rays were discovered. The first submarine was invented. The science of biology got its start. Several new chemicals and drugs were made for use in manufacturing and medicine. Sir Charles Bell began a number of studies of the human brain.

Perhaps one of the discoveries most relevant to the creation of *Frankenstein* was made in 1800, three years after Mary was born, when Alessandro Volta discovered how to produce electricity through a zinc and copper battery. Combined with Dr. Erasmus Darwin's experiment that made dead matter move, Mary Shelley had enough material to draw upon for her great experiment.

She had discovered the meaning of life—at least in the minds of the public who made it one of the most successful books of all time, a best-seller from the time it was published in 1818 right up to the present day.

The Real Frankenstein

There really is a Castle Frankenstein in Germany. Almost 800 years old, the castle is now worn with age but still possesses a haunting majesty. Photographs of the ancient castle nestled in the mountains of Germany near the Rhine can be found in Radu Florescu's fascinating book *In Search of Frankenstein.* Florescu traces the Frankenstein name back through history for nearly a thousand years to Baron von Frankenstein. The long line of

Frankenstein nobles included several prominent soldiers, writers, and political leaders.

And at least one Frankenstein was a Teutonic Knight. The Teutonic Knights were an order of warrior-monks founded in the year 1190. Originally a branch of the Knights Templar, a religious order that spearheaded European crusader armies, the Teutonic Knights soon grew into an equally powerful order. At their peak they controlled a large part of Europe, stretching from Germany and Prussia to the Baltic states.

As Florescu points out in his book, there was a point in the long history of the Frankensteins when one of them may actually have fought against someone with an equally well-known and much more sinister name—Dracula. As we'll see in another chapter, the real-life model for Bram Stoker's Dracula was a Walachian warlord named Vlad Dracul, who lived in what is now known as Romania. Since the Teutonic Knights were at war with the forces of Vlad Dracul, they may well have come face to face with one another.

Another interesting fact Florescu brings to light in his book is the existence of a scientist and alchemist named Johann Konrad Dippel, who lived for a time at Castle Frankenstein and may have been the inspiration for Mary Shelley's Victor Frankenstein. A philosopher as well as a scientist, Dippel was a well-traveled and well-learned man who tried to discover the alchemist's secret of turning lead into gold.

Many other writers have suggested that the model for Victor Frankenstein was Mary's husband, Percy. Or perhaps Lord Byron. Perhaps even both. Like the scientist portrayed in the novel, the two poets were obsessed with the challenge of creating immortal works. And like Victor Frankenstein, they often overlooked the needs of others while they conducted their grand literary experiments.

Perhaps the model for Victor Frankenstein was a combination of them all—poets, writers, scientists, noblemen—all blended into one character who was ignited with the bright spark of genius and given immortality in the pages of Mary's novel.

Darkened Dreams

The terror that haunts Victor Frankenstein through the pages of Mary Shelley's novel follows an eerie parallel path in the author's own life. The years surrounding the writing and publishing of *Frankenstein* were ones of death and loss. In March of 1815, Mary's first child died only a month after birth. Her second child was born in January of 1816, and in June she began work on the novel that would make her famous. Mary's sister committed suicide in October of the same year. Then, in early December, Mary became pregnant for a third time. In mid-December, Percy Shelley's wife, whom he was still married to, killed herself after she discovered that she was pregnant by another man. Surrounded by these gruesome events, Mary and Percy were finally married in late December of 1816.

January of 1817 began with the birth of a child to Mary's other sister. The father was Mary and Percy's friend Lord Byron. In May of 1817, *Frankenstein* was completed, and was published in 1818. Between 1818 and 1820, Mary's second and third children died. Then, in 1821, John Polidori also killed himself, two years after his book *The Vampyre* was released.

Just as Victor Frankenstein's loved ones were killed by his monstrous creation, Mary Shelley watched as those close to her fell one by one, the victims of a chilling fate. The final blow came in 1822. While Mary and Percy were living in Italy, Percy began pursuing the life of a sea captain. Always the romantic, he liked to picture himself as a man against the tide, a man who could conquer the sea.

But he was afraid of the water. He couldn't swim, and he had incredibly poor judgment when it came to sailing. On July 8, 1822, he set sail with his friend Lt. Edward Ellerker and a sailor, Charles Vivian, for a short cruise down the Italian coast. While the men were out, a sudden heavy storm erupted. Blinding rain obscured the small boat, and it was struck by a larger boat, whose captain could not see through the storm.

The boat sank, and the three men were drowned. Several days later, their bodies were washed up on shore, ravaged by the sea.

Both Percy and Mary had had premonitions and dreams about just such a death. One night, Percy had come running into Mary's room, overcome by a nightmare about his death in the sea, a death that left his body unrecognizable.

And that was how he was found by Edward John Trelawney, a British nobleman, mercenary, and sea captain. Trelawney couldn't recognize the body of his dead friend, and could only identify him by a book of poems he found in one of the drowned man's pockets.

On August 13, the bodies of Shelley and Williams were ceremoniously cremated by Trelawney, Lord Byron, and Leigh Hunt, an editor and journalist who had befriended Shelley. Shelley's

ashes were collected in a box and buried in a tomb. The words of
one of Shelley's favorite passages from Shakespeare were inscribed
on the gravestone:

Nothing of him that doth fade
But doth suffer a sea change
Into something rich and strange.

Mary Shelley found herself alone, much like the abandoned
creature of her famous novel. She went on to write five more novels. In another strange instance of art becoming life, she also
edited John Trelawney's works about his adventures, which
became very popular. Just as Mary's fictional sea captain, Robert
Walton, had chronicled the lives of Mary's Victor Frankenstein
and his creation, so did she chronicle the real-life exploits of the
man who found her husband's drowned body.

While some of Mary Shelley's other books were successful,
none ever achieved the prominence of *Frankenstein,* which has
lived on in plays, books, and movies for almost 200 years, and
which still attracts new readers.

Shorter versions of *Frankenstein* are available today, abridged
to make the language a bit easier for young readers. While many
of these edited versions capture some of the power of the story,
those who read the original novel in full will soon be swept away
by the drama of another time and place, making them feel right
at home in Mary Shelley's "castle in the air."

Chapter 2

The Headless Horseman and Friends

Gathering the Ghosts

Washington Irving had a reputation for being a dreamer—especially when he was awake. As a young boy his daydreams took him out of his New York schoolhouse and into the realm of pirates, ghosts, and early American explorers like Henry Hudson, who left his name behind on the valley in New York that Irving liked to wander through and the river that twists between its hills.

Although Irving was not the best student when he was younger, he became the first American writer whose works were admired all across Europe. Most of these writings sprang from those very same daydreams he used to get into trouble for.

But what made his work so interesting was the way he mixed his dreams with facts and legends he gathered from his early travels through Tarrytown, Sleepy Hollow, and other small villages in the Catskill Mountains. When he was a teenager, Irving journeyed through the small Catskill towns where his sister lived, talking to everyone he met—farmers, hunters, Dutch and German settlers, and veterans of the Revolutionary War. He always carried a notebook with him so that he could record every strange tale he heard and write descriptions of the forests and riverbanks he explored. Later, when he began writing his first short stories, his descriptions of the Hudson Valley were so vivid that they made his fiction seem like history.

In most of his fiction, Irving presented the characters and events as facts, even inventing imaginary scholars and professors to swear that the stories really happened. One of his most

Washington Irving

famous creations was Diedrich Knickerbocker, the name Irving often used when writing his "histories." In this way he presented a whimsical history of the early days of the United States. Later on Irving would write real histories of George Washington and Christopher Columbus that established him as one of the leading scholars and historians of his time.

Though Irving continued to write stories based on the legends and folklore he gathered during his travels in America and Europe, today he is most well known for two of the earliest stories he wrote—"Rip Van Winkle" and "The Legend of Sleepy Hollow." Both were first published in *The Sketch Book of Geoffrey Crayon, Gent.* in 1819.

At the time that Irving wrote, supernatural stories were often somber and slow-moving rehashes of the same old themes, with the authors pulling ghosts and goblins out of the woodwork like rabbits from a hat. But it was Irving who added real magic to the old legends, bringing a touch of humor and humanity to them that made them seem real.

And as Washington Irving himself, noted historian and researcher, often pointed out, these stories really happened.

Letting Sleepers Lie

Rip Van Winkle worked hard at avoiding work—as his wife was fond of telling him. He was more of a kid than the children in the small Catskill village who always followed him around to see what he was up to next, whether it was flying kites, shooting marbles, or telling ghost stories.

When he was on his own, Rip liked to go hunting and fishing or just exploring. He and his dog, Wolf, would often go wandering through the mountains to see what they could find. But one day, as dusk descended on the Catskill mountains, something found him.

As Washington Irving tells us, it happened like this: "In a long ramble on the kind of a fine autumnal day, Rip had unconsciously scrambled to one of the highest parts of the Kaatskill mountains. . . . From an opening between the trees he could overlook all the lower country for many a mile of rich woodland." From one side he could look down on the Hudson River as it wound through the highlands. "On the other side he looked down into a deep mountain glen, wild, lonely, and shagged, the bottom filled with fragments from the impending cliffs, and scarcely lighted by the reflected rays of the setting sun."

For a long time Rip Van Winkle just sat and watched the scene as if it were a play put on by nature for his own benefit. But then something stepped out from the curtain of forest, something that called his name. "Rip Van Winkle! Rip Van Winkle!— at the same time Wolf bristled up his back, and giving a low growl, skulked to his master's side, looking fearfully down into the glen."

A few moments later Rip saw a strange man, dressed in the kind of clothes that people hadn't worn for almost 200 years, climbing up the mountain. The short, stout man had bushy hair and a grizzled beard and was carrying a heavy keg of liquor on his shoulder. The man gestured for Rip to help him carry the keg. And though he was a bit frightened at first, Rip took turns with the oddly dressed man carrying the heavy keg up the mountain.

As the night grew darker and shadows fell all about them, they neared a passageway between the lofty rocks that led into a clearing from which the sound of thunder crashed and boomed. When Rip followed the man into the clearing, he saw a group of strangely dressed men playing ninepins, making loud thundering sounds as they rolled rocks across the ground to knock down the pins.

"They were dressed in a quaint, outlandish fashion; some wore short doublets, others jerkins, with long knives in their belts, and most of them had enormous breeches, of similar style with that of the guide. . . . They all had beards, of various shapes and colors."

One of the men, a stocky older man with a weather-lined face, was obviously their leader. As he studied the group, Rip realized they looked as if they'd all just stepped out of an old Flemish painting that he'd seen in one of the houses in the village. Like the men in the painting, they wore the kind of clothes people wore 200 years earlier.

The men began drinking from the keg that Rip and the short man had carried up the mountain, and Rip joined right in. The more he drank, the more his fear subsided. Soon his senses were overpowered and he fell into a deep sleep.

He woke up on the same spot on the mountain where he'd first seen the strange man carrying the keg up the hill.

But there was something strange.

Rip's beard had grown a foot long since he fell asleep. And he was stiff in the joints when he first tried to move. There was no sign of his faithful dog Wolf . . . and the well-oiled hunting rifle he carried with him had turned into a rusty old flintlock.

Confused and a bit frightened by the strangeness, Rip Van Winkle slowly made his way back to the village. And there he found out that 20 years had passed. He'd been sleeping on the mountain for two long decades.

In that time his son had grown up to look just like him.

And the sign on the tavern, which had had a picture of King George on it when Rip had last seen it, now had a painting of George Washington on it.

No one recognized him at first, but then an older woman realized he was the man who'd vanished from the village 20 years ago and greeted him by name.

Then he began telling his story. At first no one believed it—until old Peter Vanderdonk, "a descendant of the historian of that name," gave his opinion of it. Vanderdonk recognized Rip Van Winkle and, as a matter of fact, knew exactly what Rip had seen in the mountains because his father had once seen the same strange beings playing ninepins. According to Vanderdonk, "it was a fact, handed down from his ancestor the historian, that the Kaatskill mountains had always been haunted by strange beings."

These strange beings, he explained, were the ghosts of Henry Hudson and his men who had discovered the river that bore his name. He and his men returned every 20 years to keep an eye on the river and the valley. And they often were seen playing ninepins, making it sound like thunder sailing over the haunted hills.

With a man like Vanderdonk saying Rip's story had to be true, most of the other villagers soon agreed. Rip went to live with his daughter and her husband in their cottage. And often he had a chance to see his son—who looked just like him—working hard at avoiding work.

Now, since he was older and wiser and had strange stories to tell, the only work Rip really did was sit in the village tavern and tell his story to every stranger that came along. For a while he told a slightly different story every time, until finally it settled down to the exact same tale that has lasted to the present day.

As for the story's truthfulness, no less a historian than the great Diedrich Knickerbocker himself said, "I know the vicinity of our old Dutch settlements to have been very subject to marvellous events and appearances." Mr. Knickerbocker went on to say that he had personally interviewed Rip Van Winkle and found him to be a truthful man. And Knickerbocker even saw a certificate signed by a county judge stating that it was true. "The story, therefore, is beyond the possibility of doubt."

Or so says Washington Irving.

The Hills of Dream

Rip Van Winkle is one of the most well known people in fiction—or history, depending on your point of view. According to some legends there really was a man who disappeared from his Catskill village and wandered around the Hudson Valley for nearly 20 years before finally coming home. Either he'd lost his memory all that time, or he was escaping his troubles. According to this theory, Washington Irving simply wrote about a real-life person but changed some facts and added some enchanting details of his own.

Another theory holds that Rip Van Winkle is the literary descendant of European folk and fairy tales and ancient legends that Irving gathered from his travels. One such legend involved the mysterious Frederick Barbarossa, the red-bearded Holy Roman Emperor and king of Germany and Italy, who died in 1190 A.D. while setting off to fight the Third Crusade.

Barbarossa was held in such awe by the German people that they found it hard to believe he could actually die. That started a legend that Barbarossa was still alive, hidden away in a cave deep beneath the castle ruins atop Mount Kyffhausen in eastern Germany. Supposedly, Barbarossa was only sleeping, and one day would return to lead his people.

This story echoes an even earlier legend about Arthur, King of the Britons, who was carried away to Avalon after he was wounded at the battle of Camlann. Ever since King Arthur was taken there to be healed, he is said to be sleeping beneath the sacred hill of Glastonbury in England, a place many people think is Avalon, the resting place of Arthur and the Holy Grail.

Though he was a prince of a fellow, Rip Van Winkle was hardly a king—which makes a good case for Washington Irving's statement that he was just a simple and good-natured man who lived in a charming village at the foot of the Catskill Mountains.

The Haunted Historian

Although he visited an old abandoned "haunted house" by the harbor when he was a young boy, and later on gathered up ghostly tales from the Catskills, Washington Irving never really felt like he'd encountered anything ghostly. His friends swore that they'd seen ghosts, but Irving was convinced it was just shadows shifting in their imaginations.

But in a way, Irving was haunted for much of his long life. It stemmed from a tragic romance with Matilda Hoffman, a young woman he fell in love with when he was in his early 20s.

For a while Irving worked for Judge Josiah Hoffman in New York, and he became a close friend of the family. Matilda was one of the judge's daughters. And though she seemed to be shy at first, she had a sense of humor to match Irving's. The two of them fell in love and planned to be married.

But then Matilda grew sick with pneumonia. In those days diseases could often be fatal. That's what happened to Matilda. Her illness turned into tuberculosis and took her life at the age of 17.

Washington Irving stayed by her side throughout her last days. And in a way, she stayed with him for the rest of his days. He went into a long period of mourning and from then on kept her prayer book with him to keep her memory alive. "I was by her when she died," Irving wrote. "I was the last one she looked upon."

Though he lived to be 76 years old, Washington Irving never married. To help get over his mourning for Matilda, he concentrated on his writing and went on to produce haunting stories of doomed romance like "The Spectre Bridegroom."

And then there was the more down-to-earth haunting that occurred in Sleepy Hollow.

The Headless Horseman of Sleepy Hollow

Washington Irving's other famous story, "The Legend of Sleepy Hollow" has a bit more chilling side to it. Even though it has the same humorous touch as "Rip Van Winkle," the setting for this story has a haunted quality, featuring dark country roads surrounded by shape-shifting woods that move in the shadows.

It also features a tragic love affair between Ichabod Crane, the spindly schoolteacher, and Katrina Van Tassel, the prettiest girl in the village.

Washington Irving used real settings for "The Legend of Sleepy Hollow." And once again he wrote about real people. Sort of. While he gathered material for the stories from the villages of Kinderhook and Tarrytown, he created his characters from a composite of villagers he met in the area and added his own twist to the legends that filled Sleepy Hollow, which is a couple of miles away from Tarrytown. It is "one of the quietest places in the whole world. A small brook glides through it, with just murmur enough to lull one to repose. . . ."

Like most residents of Irving's stories, the people who lived in the secluded glen of Sleepy Hollow were descendants of the original Dutch settlers. They were no strangers to strange tales and were prepared to accept the rather unusual legends of the Hollow.

"A drowsy, dreamy influence seems to hang over the land. . . . Some say that the place was bewitched by a high German doctor, during the early days of the settlement; others that an old

Indian chief, the prophet or wizard of his tribe, held his pow-wows there before the country was discovered by Master Hendrick Hudson."

According to Irving, there was some bewitching power that cast a spell over Sleepy Hollow and made the inhabitants have "trances and visions; and frequently see strange sights, and hear music and voices in the air." There were haunted spots all through the Hollow.

One strange creature seemed to rule the rest of the night spirits. "It is the apparition of a figure on horseback without a head. It is said by some to be the ghost of a Hessian trooper, whose head had been carried away by a cannon-ball, in some nameless battle during the Revolutionary War." This ghostly creature haunted far and wide through the valley, but more often than not rode toward a church in Sleepy Hollow.

After introducing this strange apparition to the reader, Irving once again turns to the "experts" to prove the truthfulness of the story, citing a group of historians who collected all the facts about the trooper who lost his head.

Ever since being buried in the churchyard, the trooper galloped every night to the battlefield to search for his head. And then he rushed back through the hollow as fast as a midnight wind in order to get back to the churchyard before dawn.

Because of the Hessian trooper's eerie ride on the dark country road, "the spectre is known, at all the country firesides, by the name of the Headless Horseman of Sleepy Hollow."

And though the galloping ghost was widely known, no one had ever been hurt by him—until a schoolteacher named Ichabod Crane came to town and quickly fell in love with

Katrina Van Tassel. Not only was she one of the prettiest women in the village, she was also one of the wealthiest. Her father had a large farm with plenty of pigs and geese and apple orchards and wheat fields and corn. Ichabod could hardly wait to marry into such a well-off family. But first he had to win the heart of Katrina Van Tassel.

And Katrina had another suitor.

His name was Abraham von Brunt, but he was nicknamed Bram Bones because he was a broad-shouldered man. Though he often got into brawls, he was usually a fun-loving man, an expert horseman who led a wild crew of country boys whooping through the Hollow on midnight rides.

Before Ichabod Crane came along, Bram Bones had had no rivals for Katrina's heart. Normally this backwoods Hercules would have frightened off any other man. But Ichabod Crane was such an opposite of Bram Bones that it would have made Bram look bad if he lured Ichabod into a fight. After all, Ichabod was "tall, but exceedingly lank, with narrow shoulders, long arms and legs, hands that dangled a mile out of his sleeves, feet that might have served for shovels. . . . His head was small, and flat at top, with huge ears, large green glassy eyes, and a long snipe nose. . . ." Hardly a worthy opponent to a giant like Bram Bones. And, so it would seem, hardly the type of man Katrina would fall for. Some people believed she pretended to like Ichabod's company only to make Bram Bones jealous.

When the rivalry for Katrina's affections seemed to be turning in Ichabod's favor, Bram started to play practical jokes on Ichabod and make fun of him every chance he got.

Ichabod, who was also a singing instructor, gave Katrina

singing lessons once a week. Even though his voice was nowhere nearly as majestic as he thought, Ichabod was very proud of it. And that gave Bram one of his best ideas. He trained an old mongrel dog to whine in a hideous manner and then introduced the dog to Katrina as a singing instructor even better than Ichabod.

Despite the pranks Bram Bones and his friends played on the schoolteacher, Ichabod still seemed to be winning the contest for Katrina's heart.

Then came the night of the celebration held at Mr. Van Tassel's farm. It was the grandest occasion of the year, a feast followed by dancing and the telling of tall tales late into the night.

Ichabod was the last to leave the farm. It was close to midnight as he rode his horse through Sleepy Hollow, his mind full of the haunted stories he'd heard, his eyes full of goblin-shaped shadows everywhere he looked. And then, as the wind whistled through the trees and ghostly steps splashed in the babbling brook, Ichabod Crane saw a huge, misshapen form standing in the shadows, poised to jump at him.

Ichabod shouted into the darkness, but there was no reply. Then with a sudden bound, the dark phantom shape leaped into the middle of the road. It sat on a night-black steed, silently watching the schoolteacher. When Ichabod tried to ride slowly away, it fell in alongside him, still cloaked in shadow.

Ichabod rode faster and faster. So did the horseman. When Ichabod slowed his horse to a walk, so did the phantom rider. Finally he was able to get a good look at the rider who dogged his every move.

"On mounting a rising ground, which brought the figure of his fellow traveller in relief against the sky, gigantic in height, and muffled in a cloak, Ichabod was horror-struck, on perceiving that he was headless!—but his horror was still more increased, on observing that the head, which should have rested on his shoulders, was carried before him on the pommel of the saddle."

Ichabod Crane rode for his life then, galloping over stones that sparked in the night as the panicked horse raced for the bridge leading to the whitewashed church at the end of the hollow. As he galloped over the bridge he looked behind him to see the Headless Horseman rattling over the planks and hurling his unattached head right at the schoolteacher.

The head crashed into Ichabod's skull and knocked him into the dust. His horse ran on across the bridge and so did the goblin rider.

Ichabod's horse was found in the morning. But there was no sign of the schoolteacher.

He was never seen again in Sleepy Hollow. And though a farmer once claimed to see him in a distant part of the country working as a lawyer, most people in the valley believed that Ichabod Crane had been carried off by the Headless Horseman.

His old schoolhouse fell into decay and was rumored to be haunted by Ichabod himself. And now and then a strange singing could be heard in the hollow.

But the story ended happily for some. Bram Bones married Katrina. And soon the schoolteacher was just a pale ghost that haunted the memories of the villagers of Sleepy Hollow.

* * *

The legend of the Headless Horseman existed before Washington Irving wrote his story. Some believe it was an old Dutch or German tale that Irving rewrote and populated with American characters. But the legend also ties in with events from the Revolutionary War that were still fresh in the minds of many of the veterans Washington Irving spoke to.

During the war the American colonists had a special loathing and fear of Hessian mercenaries (German soldiers hired by the British to fight for them in America). These feelings were so strong that Americans often spoke of the Hessian troops as monsters in human form— paving the way for the road the Headless Horseman would ride. Of course, many of the Hessian mercenaries decided to fight alongside the Americans once they got here—a fact that haunted the British officers.

Another candidate for the original Headless Horseman comes from facts and folklore surrounding the early American colonies. One story reports on a British horseman known as the Phantom

Dragoon, who rode out nightly from the redcoat camp at Iron Hill, Delaware, to spy on and spook American scouts moving into the area.

Dressed in a white robe that hid his face from view, the Phantom Dragoon would race toward the American outpost at Welsh Tract Church and nearly trample the sentries who stood in his way. They fired on him but never hit him, and often would hear his eerie laughter echoing in the night as he galloped away.

But one night a skeptical old American corporal waited for the horseman behind a wooden fence, his musket aimed right at the road. When the spectral rider appeared late at night, the corporal fired head-on.

The Phantom Dragoon fell and the American sentries saw that beneath the robes he was just a brave British rider who'd been trying to scare them from the area and at the same time see how strong their defenses were. And so the Phantom Dragoon died—until the legends of the Headless Horseman and other midnight riders brought him back to life.

Irving Abroad

Washington Irving's short stories and essays made him famous in England as well as America. That was one of the reasons he was appointed as a diplomat at the American embassy in London. British society had already accepted him in the arts and was more than ready to accept him in politics.

Irving went on to make contacts with other writers, artists, and statesmen from all across Europe. He became especially fond of Spain, and on a lengthy visit there he was given access to documents and journals of Christopher Columbus and soon began writing a history of his travels. He also began writing *The Alhambra,* a collection of stories about the early days of the Moorish civilization in Spain.

Irving's next major history was about George Washington, with whom he felt a personal connection. Not only was he named after the president, but when he was six years old, Irving's nurse followed George Washington into a shop in New York City and held the young boy up to the president. George Washington touched him on the head and wished him well, something that Irving never forgot.

After years of traveling and working for the U.S. government as a diplomat, Washington Irving returned to his home at Sunnyside near Tarrytown and devoted the rest of his life to writing. There he finished the last volume in his history of George Washington. He lived to be 76 years old, and when he died, he was buried in the cemetery at the Sleepy Hollow Church.

And there he lies today. Or maybe, like some of the characters he wrote about, he's only sleeping, waiting until it's time to come back and tell a few more legends about Sleepy Hollow.

Chapter

3

The Master
of Saranac

Robert Louis Stevenson

The Cabinet of Dr. Jekyll

Robert Louis Stevenson found a monster in his closet.

It was a wooden cabinet crafted by the hands of Deacon William Brodie, a respected gentleman of Edinburgh whose life ended swinging from a gallows pole. Before he was caught and hanged as the leader of a band of thieves who prowled the streets at night, Deacon Brodie was considered one of the finest architects and craftsmen in Scotland.

When Stevenson was a young boy the cabinet occupied a corner of his room—much as the true tale of Deacon Brodie would occupy a corner of his mind for most of his life, before bursting through the doors of his imagination in the form of *The Strange Case of Dr. Jekyll and Mr. Hyde,* one of the finest horror novels ever written.

Jekyll and Hyde was not the first novel Stevenson wrote. By the time it appeared in 1886, the same year another of his well-known books, *Kidnapped,* was published, he'd already written *Treasure Island,* which had established him as a master of the adventure novel. And his book *A Child's Garden of Verses* had already shown him to be a man with a sense of humor and wit.

But *Jekyll and Hyde* was quite a departure from his other works. It hardly seemed like the kind of book to come from the pen of such a good-natured man. In fact, the novel was so far ahead of its time that it could hardly be expected to come from anyone's pen. As a result, this unique horror tale made Stevenson famous around the world.

In this novel Stevenson created one of the most unique monsters in literature. The world had already shuddered to *Franken-stein*, and *Dracula* was waiting in the wings. But these hideous creatures paled beside the evil monster Stevenson devised. For Stevenson's monster was *man himself*.

There are two main characters in the novel: Dr. Jekyll, a fine upstanding London gentleman born to wealth, and Mr. Hyde, a thrill-seeking scoundrel who stalks the streets at night with an aura of evil settling about him.

Mr. Hyde is a truly frightening man, who thinks nothing of trampling a young child underfoot or murdering an old man just to see what it would be like. But the most frightening thing about Mr. Hyde is that he has another identity—Dr. Jekyll. During the daytime Dr. Jekyll is a hardworking chemist, a well-respected man in town. But at night he turns into Mr. Hyde by taking a strange potion he invented.

The first time Jekyll swallows the potion, he finds that it changes not only his personality, but his physical features as well. "The most racking pangs succeeded: a grinding in the bones, deadly nausea, and a horror in the spirit that cannot be exceeded at the hour of birth or death."

The now-transformed chemist runs to a mirror to see not the old face of Dr. Jekyll, but a new face looking back at him. "Evil was written broadly and plainly on the face of the other. . . . And yet when I looked upon that ugly idol in the glass, I was conscious of no repugnance, rather of a leap of welcome."

For several years the good Dr. Jekyll has lived the kind of conservative life-style expected of him by his peers in high society. When he takes the potion, he thinks he's free at last to live another kind of life. But he soon realizes he's not free at all and is in fact a prisoner of evil. The drug makes him a slave to his evil side—a side that grows stronger all the time, like a shadow hanging over his life.

Stevenson's novel shows us the characters of Jekyll and Hyde through the eyes of a lawyer named Mr. Utterson and of Dr. Lanyon, both old friends of Dr. Jekyll who are disturbed by the changes coming over him. Only when it's too late do they realize that Jekyll and Hyde are one and the same man.

We also see Mr. Hyde through the eyes of Dr. Jekyll himself, who naturally witnesses the crimes committed by his evil alter ego. When he is in his right mind, that of Dr. Jekyll, he tries to prevent the transformation from happening. But the personality of Hyde has grown so strong that soon Dr. Jekyll becomes the shadow personality and Hyde the main personality.

Mr. Utterson first hears of the evil Mr. Hyde when he and his friend Enfield walk down a bright, clean London street that leads to a run-down area with a sinister feel to it. Enfield points out a door in a courtyard that has an unusual story to it.

Long past midnight on a dark winter morning Enfield saw an unusual man stumble around a corner into a young girl. Rather than help her up, Enfield said, "the man trampled calmly over the child's body and left her screaming on the ground." The man would have simply walked away if Enfield and other people from the street hadn't come to the screaming girl's rescue.

"It wasn't like a man; it was like some damned juggernaut. . . . He gave me one look, so ugly that it brought out the sweat on me like running." While a crowd gathered around Hyde, he stared back at them "with a kind of black, sneering coolness."

Since the girl wasn't seriously hurt, the crowd decided to let Mr. Hyde go if he could pay damages of 100 pounds. Hyde vanished through the door, then returned with gold coins and a check for the remaining balance. It was a check from Dr. Jekyll's bank account.

Upon hearing this story, Utterson decides to find out what possible connection there could be between his friend Dr. Jekyll and this loathsome Mr. Hyde. Something else is bothering Mr. Utterson. For he is Jekyll's lawyer, and knows that the doctor's will has a strange clause in it. In case Dr. Jekyll vanishes, the will leaves all of his fortune to the despicable Mr. Hyde.

From that point on, the lawyer haunts the area around the mysterious doorway until finally he sees Mr. Hyde for himself. "It was a fine dry night; frost in the air; the streets as clean as a ballroom floor, the lamps, unshaken by any wind, drawing a regular pattern of light and shadow." After hearing scuttling footsteps around the corner, Utterson sees Hyde face to face.

"Mr. Hyde was pale and dwarfish, he gave an impression of deformity without any nameable malformation . . . and he spoke with a husky, whispering, and somewhat broken voice." Almost as important as the physical characteristics of Mr. Hyde is the impression that Utterson gets from being near him. "The man seems hardly human! Something troglodytic . . . or is it the mere radiance of a foul soul?"

Utterson's sense of dread upon seeing Hyde contrasts with his impressions of his good friend Dr. Jekyll, who is a "large, well-made smooth-faced man of fifty, with something of a slyish cast perhaps, but every mark of capacity and kindness." Dr. Jekyll is a

direct opposite, physically and morally, of Mr. Hyde—even though they are the same person.

Stevenson's novel about the good and evil nature that can exist in one person and about how drugs can unleash that evil had several influences. But as we mentioned in the beginning of this chapter, one of the main influences was a real-life Jekyll-and-Hyde called Deacon William Brodie.

William Brodie died nearly 100 years before Stevenson wrote *The Strange Case of Dr. Jekyll and Mr. Hyde*. But Stevenson was definitely familiar with the case of Deacon Brodie.

As a young man Stevenson studied law at Edinburgh University, although his real schooling came in the streets of Edinburgh, where he walked in the footsteps of Deacon Brodie as well as the notorious grave robbers Burke and Hare, who inspired his horror story "The Body Snatchers." Realizing where his future lay, he left law for literature and embarked on a dazzling career as a journalist, poet, essayist, and novelist.

His fascination with the dual personality of Deacon Brodie, who lived on High Street in Stevenson's native Edinburgh, led him to write a play about him called *Deacon Brodie, or the Double Life*.

Like Dr. Jekyll, Brodie was a fine, upstanding gentleman. He was a skilled architect and carpenter who was welcomed into some of the finest homes of Edinburgh. During the day he was a well-spoken and well-dressed man who knew how to get along in all levels of society.

But at night Brodie turned into a thrill-seeking robber who broke into some of the very same mansions he visited during the daytime as a guest. His personality was so different that it was as if the fall of night had colored his soul dark.

Brodie led a pack of thieves from the lower classes of society who looked upon him as their natural leader—for he knew how to get along with them, too. A gambler, drinker, robber, and rogue, he lived for the nighttime, when he could steal to his heart's content.

Unfortunately for Brodie, he wasn't content for long. Night after night he directed his band of thieves, stealing more and more, until finally the police of Edinburgh caught him in the act. After a brief escape, he was captured by the police, fittingly enough, hiding inside a cabinet.

As Stevenson would later write, one of the key inspirations for *The Strange Case of Dr. Jekyll and Mr. Hyde* was an amazingly detailed dream in which "a man was being pressed into a cabinet, where he swallowed a drug and changed into another being."

The Dream Engineers

Robert Louis Stevenson was a dreamer. Even while he was awake his mind often sowed the fields of dreams, harvesting and shaping the strange and wonderful ideas sowed by "the Little People," spirits whom he believed worked all night while he slept, fashioning stories for him in the brightly lit theater of his mind.

He saw no limits in his dreams or in his life. Though he had had a respiratory disease since birth, Stevenson didn't let that stop him. He traveled across Europe, sometimes working his way up and down river by canoe. He crossed the ocean on freighters, then crossed the American plains by train. He finally traveled to the South Pacific, where he became the storyteller for a tribe of islanders who adopted him as one of their own. Just like one of the adventurers in his novels *Treasure Island, Kidnapped, The Black Arrow,* and *The Master of Ballantrae,* he'd gone out into the world and brought back its treasures—in glittering gems of fiction.

Those who knew him described Robert Louis Stevenson as a modest and gentle man with a great sense of humor and charm. Though he claimed not to take himself or his work too seriously, the artistry and craft in Stevenson's work is rarely matched by modern writers. In less than a hundred pages, *Dr. Jekyll and Mr. Hyde* gives the reader a chilling and fascinating look at characters who can never be forgotten.

One reason Stevenson's short novel had such a lasting impact was Stevenson's ability to conjure up striking images. In one scene Dr. Jekyll is sitting on a park bench in the middle of a beautiful wintry day. "I sat in the sun on a bench, the animal within me licking the chops of memory; the spiritual side a little drowsed." Suddenly he looks down to see his hand transforming into the hairy, apelike hand of Mr. Hyde. Not only is he changing into Hyde without even taking the potion, but now, as Hyde, he is a hunted man wanted for killing an elderly man on the street.

This ability to create startling images and strange situations for his characters to confront originated in Stevenson's dreams. He often wrote about the very detailed dreams that made him feel like an actor in an unfinished play performed on a strangely lit stage in his mind. Using his dreams as a starting point, he fashioned these plays into logical stories. In fact, reading *The Strange Case of Dr. Jekyll and Mr. Hyde* is almost like stepping into one of

Robert Louis Stevenson's dreams. You can almost hear the shuffling footsteps of Mr. Hyde as he walks the London streets at night.

There is one particular picture of Robert Louis Stevenson that best captures the mischievous spirit of the dreamer in him. It is the picture at the beginning of this chapter.

Stevenson looks right at the viewer from his photograph, almost like one of those portraits in haunted houses where the eyes seem to follow you wherever you go. His eyes are direct but sly, almost as if they're saying, Wait until you hear this one; almost as if he is as amazed by the story he is about to tell as the reader will be.

His hair is a bit long in the picture and he's wearing a black velvet jacket, looking like a bohemian artist who would be at home in any era. He's sporting a handlebar mustache that makes him look something like a gunslinger. Or in his case, a word-slinger, a rapid-fire creator of images who never runs out of ammunition.

Perhaps that was because of his dreams. If he couldn't create a story on his own, he would often look for ideas in the pages of his dreams. In his article "A Chapter on Dreams," Stevenson wrote how he often found himself reading strange books in his dreams. Or how he was an observer of incredibly detailed dramas, as if he were sitting in the audience of his dream theater while his Little People went to work spinning stories for him.

In the beginning these Little People often presented the sleeping Stevenson with unusual images that always stayed with him but couldn't really fit into a story. For example, in one dream

Stevenson was alone in a hillside farmhouse, looking out the window. He was all alone except for an old brown retriever sleeping against the outside wall of the house. Suddenly the dog reached out, caught a fly with his paw, and popped it into his mouth, then looked up at Stevenson and winked at him.

End of dream. End of story. Stevenson could find nothing to do with the dream dog—who followed him around in his memory forever after but never found a place in a story. According to Stevenson this was a result of the Little People's inexperience in crafting full-length tales. As he became a more experienced writer, Stevenson found that the Little People in his dreams got better at providing him with stories that made enough sense so that when he was awake he could actually shape them into salable and entertaining pieces of fiction.

Before going to sleep Stevenson would often try to think up fantastic stories. Then when he passed into dreamland the Little People picked up the threads of his imagination and wove them into stories. "And, behold!" Stevenson wrote, "at once the Little People begin to bestir themselves in the same quest, and labour all night long, and all night long set before [me] truncheons of tales upon their lighted theatre."

Though he writes about the Little People in a humorous way, Stevenson makes it clear that he regards the land of dream as a territory populated by creatures of the imagination, Little People or Brownies who go off on their own to dream up their stories.

"Who are the Little People?" Stevenson asks. "They are near connections of the dreamer's . . . only I think they have more talent; and one thing is beyond doubt, they can tell him a story piece by piece, like a serial, and keep him all the while in ignorance of where they aim."

Stevenson then writes that the Little People are "just my Brownies, God bless them! who do one-half my work for me while I am fast asleep, and in all human likelihood, do the rest for me as well, when I am wide awake and fondly suppose I do it for myself."

As an example of how his dreams shaped his fiction, Stevenson explained that he was trying to think up a story about a man with a dual personality but couldn't find the right way to tell it. After two days of racking his brain for a plot, Stevenson found it in a dream.

"On the second night I dreamed the scene at the window, and a scene afterward split in two, in which Hyde, pursued for some crime, took the powder and underwent the change in the presence of his pursuers."

Fanny, his wife, woke him up when she heard him cry out from the dream—or nightmare. Upset that she had interrupted such a fine tale, Stevenson quickly went back to sleep in order to finish the story. According to this anecdote, Stevenson then woke up in the morning and wrote *Jekyll and Hyde* in three days. His wife supposedly found it so shocking and lacking in moral that he burned it and started all over again, once more turning out the story in three days.

It is hard to imagine a writer from any era throwing out any novel and starting over from scratch. So perhaps this is just a bit of fantasy surrounding an already fantastic tale. It's certainly possible that Stevenson put aside the first draft of *Jekyll and Hyde* and used it as a guide for his second version, which might account for its short length but long-lasting imagery.

This second version definitely had a moral that is as valid today as it was when he wrote it. Under the influence of a drug he thinks is the perfect escape from his problems, Dr. Jekyll steps into a horror he cannot escape. His humanity fades as the drug brings out the evil in him and cuts him off from his friends, turning him into a wasted creature that preys on society.

In the end Dr. Jekyll is barely able to hang on to his original identity, knowing that if he waits any longer Mr. Hyde will take over forever. Jekyll finds himself wondering if Mr. Hyde—just like the real-life Deacon Brodie—will die hanging from the gallows for his crime.

The last act of Dr. Jekyll is to prepare one more potion that will kill Hyde if he takes it. As Dr. Jekyll writes in the end, "This, then, is the last time, short of a miracle, that Henry Jekyll can think his own thoughts or see his own face (now how sadly altered!) in the glass. . . . Here then, as I lay down the pen and proceed to seal up my confession, I bring the life of that unhappy Henry Jekyll to an end."

Jekyll changes one last time into Mr. Hyde, and in that desolate, corrupt form, Jekyll's old friend Utterson finds him dead on the floor. The end has come for them both.

The American Spirit

Robert Louis Stevenson and his wife came to America in 1887 and moved into a cottage in Saranac Lake, New York. They'd come to the small village in the middle of the Adirondacks for the crisp mountain air, which was supposed to be beneficial to tuberculosis sufferers such as Stevenson.

In Saranac he wrote *The Master of Ballantrae,* a stirring adventure novel that once again proved him an unmatched master of fiction. And while he was there he no doubt came upon the ghostly legend of Duncan Campbell, another Scotsman who'd come to the haunting and majestic spires of the Adirondack woods.

He captured the story of Duncan Campbell in an epic poem called *Ticonderoga: A Legend of the West Highlands,* which appeared in *Scribner's Magazine* in 1887.

This poem traces the real-life journey of Duncan Campbell, a Scottish major in the 42d Regiment, known as the Black Watch. Several years before Campbell came to America to fight in the French and Indian War, the ghost of his recently murdered cousin Donald appeared in Campbell's castle at Inverawe and promised they would meet again at Ticonderoga. Duncan shrugged off the visitation because the name Ticonderoga meant nothing to him—until July 8, 1758, when his regiment marched north through the Adirondacks toward the French army at Fort Carillon. And then he found out the Indian name for the fort—*Ticonderoga.* He met his cousin's ghost once more and joined him shortly thereafter when he was mortally wounded in the battle of Ticonderoga.

The real-life story was perfect for Robert Louis Stevenson, whose imaginative account captures the mystery surrounding the supernatural soldier. One passage shows the Highlander's sense of dread as the battle approaches. Speaking to one of the Indian warriors fighting at his side, he says:

For many shall fall the morn,
But I shall fall with the first.
O, you of the outland tongue,
You of the painted face,
This is the place of my death;
Can you tell me the name of the place?

The warrior explains that the fort has a much older name than the one the French know it by.

"It went by another word,"
Quoth he of the shaven head:
"It was called Ticonderoga
In the days of the great dead."

Though he didn't live in Saranac for long, Stevenson left a lasting impression. Today his cottage is a museum where visitors can walk through the rooms where he dreamed his dreams.

Stevenson followed his dreams across America and then sailed to the South Pacific, where he and his wife settled in the Samoan Islands. He stayed there until the end of his life in 1894, when he died suddenly of a stroke.

But although he died in a strange land, he didn't die as a stranger. The islanders were so enchanted by the wonderful tales he'd spun for them that they accepted him as one of their own. Robert Louis Stevenson became known throughout Samoa as Tusitala, the native word for "storyteller."

Chapter

4

*Will the Real
Vampire Please
Stand Up?*

Son of Dracula

"The mouth, so far as I could see it under the heavy moustache, was fixed and rather cruel-looking, with peculiarly sharp white teeth; these protruded over the lips, whose remarkable ruddiness showed astonishing vitality in a man of his years . . . the chin was broad and strong, and the cheeks firm though thin. . . ."

This is the face that looks at Jonathan Harker as he and Count Dracula sit before the flickering light of a fireplace in Castle Dracula. Dracula has summoned the young British lawyer to his castle in the rugged mountains of Transylvania to help him purchase some property in England.

Soon after his arrival, Harker realizes his chances of leaving the castle alive are slim. The count and three mysterious women in the castle study him like wild animals looking at their prey. In fact, when Harker and the count hear ferocious wolves howling outside the castle, Dracula smiles and says "Listen to them—the children of the night. What music they make!"

* * *

Count Dracula is one of the most infamous monsters ever to haunt the literary landscape. Ever since Bram Stoker's novel *Dracula* first appeared in 1897, the white-fanged, blood-drinking vampire has lived on in plays, novels, comics, and movies.

But not quite as well known as Stoker's vampire is the real-life Transylvanian prince whose monstrous deeds in the 1400s gave birth to the legend of the vampire described in Stoker's book. In many ways the real Transylvanian prince was more of a monster than anything that Bram Stoker could dream up on his own.

Like many horror writers, Bram Stoker said the idea for *Dracula* came to him in a frightful dream—about a vampire king rising from his tomb. But aside from the dream, Stoker had a lot of factual inspiration for his story.

While working as the stage manager for famous British actor Henry Irving, Bram Stoker met a professor from Hungary named Arminius Vambery, who was familiar with the real-life story of the cruel medieval prince who ruled Walachia, now a part of Romania.

Stoker's imagination was captured by the strange tale. With a sense of drama honed by years of working in London's Lyceum Theatre, he seized upon the facts of this horrible prince and added just enough fantasy to make his character a literary son of the real-life monster.

The Horrifying History of Vlad Dracul

The amazing transformation of man into vampire began in the late 1400s, when a Transylvanian warlord named Vlad Dracul led his knights beneath a strange banner. As the men on horseback galloped over the Walachian countryside, the banner snapped in the wind, making it look as if the creature on the banner were actually flying. It was a dragon with wings.

Vlad Dracul was a knight of the Order of the Dragon. And under that banner he fought the Turkish armies that often invaded his land. Sometimes he also fought the neighboring

Hungarian armies, although he just as often was allied with them. Like his father, who was also named Vlad Dracul, he was forever caught in the middle between larger countries with larger armies and always had to be ready for war from any side. As a mark of respect for his father, he added an "a" to Dracul and was also known as Dracula, or Son of the Dragon.

Outnumbered on all sides, Dracula decided to use one weapon that would strike at his enemies whenever they heard his name. The weapon was terror. He wanted to make people fear to come into his country, to make them shudder whenever they heard his name. He did this by killing enemy soldiers in such horrible ways that the armies wouldn't want to set foot in the Walachian warlord's territory.

After one battle, Dracula killed nearly 20,000 defeated invading soldiers by impaling them on long stakes set into the ground—a cruel form of execution that often took days to result in death. Dracula left the stakes standing across the countryside, a forest of corpses to remind his enemies of what happened to those who fought against him. This horrible deed earned Dracula the name Vlad the Impaler, and it caused his name to be feared all across Europe.

Unfortunately for his own people, Dracula also executed many of them in the same manner. Some were members of the ruling class of nobles who plotted to remove him from the throne. But many were simply people who said the wrong thing or wore the wrong clothes in his presence. One time when ambassadors from another country failed to take off their hats in front of him, he had the hats nailed to their heads.

Although he often rewarded peasants for bravery, those who

Bram Stoker

The Vampyre, devised by Lord Byron and John Polidori at the same time and place where Mary Shelley dreamed up Frankenstein in 1816.

So-called factual stories about vampires were also available. Many German and Hungarian pamphlets about "real-life" vampires had been published as early as the 1500s. Among the books Stoker could have studied about historical vampires in Eastern Europe was one called *Dissertation on Vampires* written in 1759, which recorded accounts written by officers stationed in Walachia that listed dragoons who were supposedly killed by vampires.

Though Dracula wasn't the first fictional vampire, he was and is the longest lived. Stoker combined just enough history and geography of Romania with his own imaginary history to create a believable prince of the undead.

Jonathan Harker's trip through the Transylvanian countryside at the beginning of the novel gives the reader a quick lesson in the harsh geography of the land—and then begins a long lesson in terror that starts as soon as he enters the castle.

"A key was turned with the loud grating noise of long disuse, and the great door swung back."

When Count Dracula first welcomes Harker into the castle, he seems to be an older man with a white mustache, clad from head to toe in black. But the count shakes hands with an iron grip that is as cold as ice, "more like the hand of a dead than a living man." Soon Harker learns that the count's appearance can change quite drastically. Another time when Harker sees the count, he appears to be much younger and stronger—almost as if there's some new blood in him.

His encounters with Dracula grow increasingly stranger. When Dracula appears behind Harker while he is shaving, his image doesn't show up in the mirror Harker is looking into. Then, when Harker cuts himself, the count's eyes blaze with demonic fury and hunger at the sight of blood.

Dracula then has Harker write letters back home to England saying that he's already left the castle. Fearing that he'll never make it back to England to see his fiancée, Mina, again, Harker starts looking for a way to escape. But then he sees what happens to another one of Dracula's victims when she comes to the castle looking for her missing child. The count summons wolves from the forest, who tear her to pieces.

Even before Harker can risk facing the wolves, he has to find a way out of the castle. The room he's locked into looks out on the steep side of the castle, with a sheer drop below. One thing is certain—he can't climb from the window the same way he sees Dracula do: "I saw the whole man slowly emerge from the window and begin to crawl down the castle wall over that dreadful abyss, *face down,* with his cloak spreading out around him like great wings." He moved "with considerable speed, just as a lizard moves along a wall."

Since Harker never sees Dracula during the daytime, he figures that's the best time for him to look for a way out. Climbing out his window he scales the wall down to Dracula's window and slips into his room. There he finds a heap of Roman, British, Austrian, Hungarian, Greek, and Turkish gold coins in one corner of the room, all of them 300 years old or older. He also finds a door that leads down a steep stone staircase to a crypt full of long wooden boxes filled with soil.

In one of the boxes lies Dracula. "He was either dead or asleep, I could not say which—for the eyes were open and stony, but without the glassiness of death—and the cheeks had the warmth of life through all their pallor; the lips were as red as ever. But there was no sign of movement, no pulse, no breath, no beating of the heart."

But even from those dead-seeming eyes burns a look of hatred. Sensing the presence of great evil, Harker panics and escapes back up to his own room. The next time he visits the crypt, Harker sees a young-looking Dracula, his white hair and moustache now turned a dark iron gray, his cheeks full, and his lips red with gouts of blood. Overcome with hatred for the leech-like vampire, Harker grabs a shovel and swings for his head. . . .

"But as I did so the head turned, and the eyes fell full upon me, with all their blaze of basilisk horror. The sight seemed to paralyse me, and the shovel turned in my hand and glanced from the face, merely making a deep gash above the forehead."

The shovel falls from his hands and then he hears the approach of the Gypsies Dracula has summoned to drive him away from the castle for the first leg of his journey to England. Harker races back to his room and then begins a treacherous escape down from the steep castle walls.

After a long, dangerous journey through the countryside, Harker finally reunites with Mina in Budapest and marries her. They return home to England to find that Dracula is alive and well.

Even before reaching England Dracula has had his fill of blood, as one by one the sailors on board his ship became his victims. By the time the ship runs aground on the British coast, only the captain is left, tied to the mast of the ship. And then, in the form of an immense dog, Dracula runs away from the ship of the dead.

One of his first victims in England is a friend of Mina's named Lucy Westenra, who wastes away after Dracula drinks her blood. She becomes a vampire herself and nightly rises from her coffin—until, with the help of vampire hunter Dr. Van Helsing, her fiancé drives a stake through her heart to release her from the vampire's curse.

The next victim is Mina herself, who is attacked by Dracula after he changes his shape from an eerie mist back into his vampire form. Now Mina is slowly becoming a vampire. Unless Count Dracula himself is killed, she will soon become one of his vampire slaves.

Jonathan Harker joins forces with Dr. Van Helsing and Lucy's fiancé to hunt for the vampire. Knowing that Dr. Van Helsing understands how to kill vampires, Dracula flees. The chase leads back to Transylvania.

Dr. Van Helsing gets to the castle first. Since it's still daylight he finds the three vampire women sleeping in their coffins and kills them one by one.

Soon afterward, near sundown, Harker and an American named Quincey Morris finally catch up to the wagon that is carrying Dracula back to his castle in a coffin-shaped box full of earth. They fight their way through Dracula's Gypsy escort and then open up the coffin.

Mina, who arrives with Van Helsing just as the final battle begins, sees Count Dracula one last time: "I saw the Count lying within the box upon the earth, some of which the rude falling from the cart had scattered over him. He was deathly pale, just like a waxen image, and the red eyes glared with the horrible vindictive look which I knew too well.

"As I looked, the eyes saw the sinking sun, and the look of hate in them turned to triumph."

Before the vampire can rise, Harker and Morris slash down at him with their knives. Harker's long curved kukei knife cuts off his head and the American's bowie knife stakes him through the heart.

"It was like a miracle; but before our very eyes, and almost in the drawing of a breath, the whole body crumbled into dust and passed from our sight."

The wolves that had been howling all around suddenly vanish into the woods along with the Gypsy escort. But more blood has been shed. Quincey Morris falls dead of a knife wound he received when he and Harker had to fight their way to the coffin. But even though it led to his death, Morris is glad that he had a chance to help in the victory over the undead vampire lord. With the vampire returned to dust, Mina is free once again.

And there the story ends.

Bram Stoker wrote many other horror stories, but today is remembered mainly for *Dracula.*

That novel set the stage for many other writers who embellished on the themes Stoker established. But none have had quite the same impact as *Dracula*. Aside from the horrifying sight of the vampire lord, one of the more frightening themes of the novel is the idea that evil can take so many different forms.

Dracula could transform himself into a wolflike beast. Or he could fly to impossible heights in the shape of a bat. And he could also travel in the form of a misty apparition, undetected until he resumed his vampire form.

Another frightening thing about the vampires was the lasting effect they had on their victims. People you loved could turn into monsters you feared. Mina's friend Lucy became a vampire and Mina herself was in danger of becoming one—not exactly the best way for a bride to start out her marriage.

But thanks to Harker's courage and Bram Stoker's imagination, they lived happily ever after. *Dracula* is nearly a hundred years old, and so far his characters still show every sign of life.

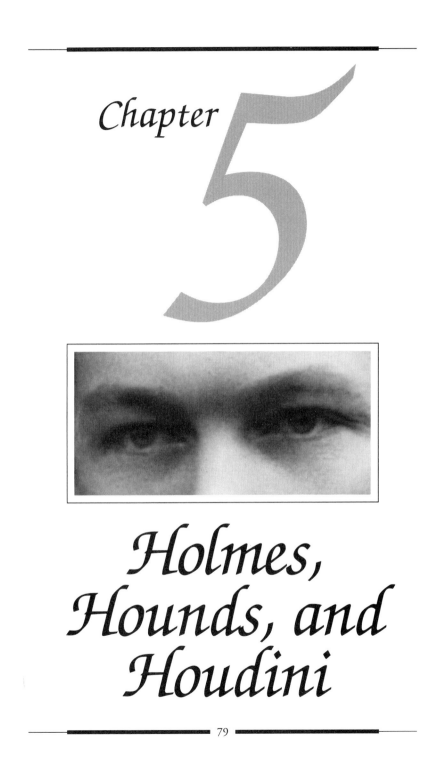

Chapter 5

Holmes, Hounds, and Houdini

Fate and the Physician

Sherlock Holmes first came to life in a short novel that appeared in the pages of a British magazine called *Beeton's Christmas Annual.* It was 1887, and by then Arthur Conan Doyle had published several supernatural stories, but had achieved no real fame.

Initially the same thing happened with the Sherlock Holmes novel. It would be a few more years before his short stories about the great detective would gain him a worldwide following. At the time, Doyle believed his best chance for a successful career remained in the field of medicine.

Doyle was a well-trained doctor who had gained valuable experience working as a ship's doctor on voyages to the Arctic and then to Africa before he began his practice back in England. After sharing offices with a friend from medical school, he had set up his own small practice in Southsea. Since it really wasn't busy enough in Southsea for him to make a profitable living, in 1890 he and his wife moved to London, where he hoped to increase the number of his patients.

But he soon found there wasn't a worldwide rush for his services. He rented offices at 2 Devonshire Place, an area where many successful doctors had their practices. There it was that Doyle set up shop as an eye doctor. But he saw no patients.

As he wrote in his *Memoirs and Adventures,* "Every morning I walked from the lodgings, at Montague Place, reached my consulting-room at ten and sat there until three or four, with never a ring to disturb my serenity."

Without any patients to take up his time, Doyle turned to his writing again and began producing more Sherlock Holmes stories. These short stories all appeared in the pages of *The Strand Magazine,* a popular showcase for many of the best writers of the day. The stories made their way across the Atlantic and were published in America, starting a craze for the great detective that is still going strong to this day.

As Doyle achieved fame in both England and the United States, the income from writing those short stories gave him the incentive to quit his medical practice and make his living totally as a writer.

"It was as well," he wrote, "for not one single patient had ever crossed the threshold of my room."

Clues to the Character

The real Sherlock Holmes carried a scalpel instead of a magnifying glass.

His name was Dr. Joseph Bell, and he was a surgeon and instructor at Edinburgh University in Scotland. With a single glance he could often tell what people did for a living or where they were from.

One of the students who noticed Bell's ability to find clues where no one else could was Arthur Conan Doyle, who would later give his famous fictional detective, Sherlock Holmes, the same skills. As an assistant to Bell, Doyle had plenty of time to observe this medical "detective" at work. Years later, when Doyle went about creating his master detective, he had a good idea of how he would act and look.

"Sherlock Holmes was pacing up and down the platform, his tall, gaunt figure made even gaunter and taller by his long grey travelling cloak and close-fitting cloth cap."

Doyle made Holmes more than just a tall and spare mysterious figure by lending him some of his own characteristics—an intense curiosity, a wide-ranging knowledge of unusual facts, and an eagerness to face challenges head-on. As a young schoolboy, Doyle took up sports as well as the pen, becoming a skilled soccer player and boxer. Though the lean, hawk-faced Holmes was physically different from the broad-shouldered Doyle, he, too, was a skilled fighter. In one story Holmes is revealed to be a master of baritsu, a Japanese martial art so rare that to this day it has never been heard of outside of Doyle's fiction. Obviously both Doyle and Holmes were equipped with powerful imaginations.

In some ways, Doyle borrowed a few traits from Holmes. Long after Doyle became a famous author and could have lived a life of luxury, he actually did some real-life detective work and solved cases that had previously resulted in the wrong people being put into jail. In the case of Mr. Edaliji, who served three years in jail for allegedly killing and mutilating some livestock, Doyle proved that Edaliji was not physically capable of the act. Since Doyle had training as an eye doctor, he recognized that Edaliji's impaired vision prevented him from even getting to the site where the crime was committed—let alone evading pursuit. Doyle cleared the man's name and also identified the real culprit, but the small-town authorities had no desire to reopen the case.

Another innocent man named Oscar Slater spent almost 20 years in a Glasgow, Scotland, prison for allegedly murdering an elderly woman in 1908—until Doyle launched a crusade to set

Sir Arthur Conan Doyle

him free. This time Doyle proved that even though the witnesses had identified another man as the killer, the Glasgow police made them change their story and pin the murder on Slater, an American who was just about to leave Scotland. Although Slater was released from prison, the authorities made no effort to find the real killer.

In both of these cases, Arthur Conan Doyle performed as well as Sherlock Holmes himself. And Doyle could have done even more detective work if he had wanted. His mail was full of letters addressed to Sherlock Holmes, asking if the detective would take on some of their cases.

This amused and bemused Doyle. Though he enjoyed the success of the Sherlock Holmes stories, it was discomforting to find out that so many people actually thought Holmes really existed. Doyle considered Sherlock Holmes a minor achievement compared to some of his other works. All through the period he wrote the Sherlock Holmes stories he also wrote historical novels, adventure and horror stories, and nonfiction books. Since spiritualism was one of his major interests throughout his life, Doyle wrote *The History of Spiritualism* and other books on the subject. He also wrote an account of the Boer War, which he had seen firsthand.

When war broke out in 1899 Doyle volunteered his services as a doctor and set up a hospital in Cape Town for the British troops who were fighting Dutch settlers in South Africa. It was this tour of duty that earned him a knighthood in 1902, which is why he is also known as Sir Arthur Conan Doyle. Once Doyle decided on the right course of action, he followed it no matter how much trouble it brought him.

His belief in the supernatural would later cause Doyle great controversy, winning him fans in the ranks of spiritualists, but subjecting him to criticism by the more down-to-earth admirers of his Sherlock Holmes stories. But Doyle was such a sincere, likable man that even though many people considered his supernatural beliefs to be naive and he himself to be gullible, they still held him in high regard. His fervent belief in spirit photography, séances, and mediums who were proven to be frauds was looked upon as the eccentric behavior of an otherwise brilliant man.

Ironically, it was this same interest in the supernatural that inspired one of his most famous Sherlock Holmes novels.

The Haunted Hound

While Doyle wrote many chilling supernatural stories, he achieved one of his most haunting effects with a more down-to-earth monster in *The Hound of the Baskervilles*. Like all of the Sherlock Holmes stories, this one is narrated by Dr. Watson, a retired British army doctor with all of the virtues Holmes required—intelligence, courage, good humor, and the ability to put up with the often self-absorbed detective.

But in this celebrated case, Holmes and Watson are taken out of the familiar cozy environment of 221B Baker Street in London and cast upon one of England's cold and haunting moors. They are out to solve the murder of Sir Charles Baskerville, the latest member of the family to die from the legendary Baskerville curse.

The man who enlists Sherlock Holmes to investigate Charles's

death is Dr. James Mortimer, a friend and neighbor of the family. Mortimer comes to London to explain the strange circumstances of Baskerville's death and read to Holmes an old family document about a cursed hound that plagues the Baskervilles. Along with investigating the death of his friend, Mortimer also wants Holmes to protect Henry Baskerville, the heir of the family estate, who is on his way from Canada.

According to some of the people who live by the moor, a great beast has recently been seen there. They describe it as a "huge creature, luminous, ghastly, and spectral." This beast is similar to the hellhound of the Baskerville legend.

The legend begins with the first Hugo Baskerville, who sees a beautiful young woman and kidnaps her so that he can marry her. When she manages to escape from the drunken Hugo, he orders his men to send the dogs after her.

Hugo saddles his horse and rides ahead of the others, eager to track down the helpless woman.

A short time later three of Hugo's companions find both him and the girl lifeless on the moor. The girl is dead from fatigue and fright. But Hugo has met a much grislier fate.

"Standing over Hugo, and plucking at his throat, there stood a foul thing, a great, black beast, shaped like a hound, yet larger than any hound that ever mortal eye has rested upon. And even as they looked the thing tore the throat out of Hugo Baskerville, on which, as it turned its blazing eyes and dripping jaws upon them, the three shrieked with fear and rode for dear life, still screaming, across the moor."

Ever since that time the descendants of Hugo Baskerville were said to be haunted by the spectral beast, and many of them died mysterious deaths. The legend was written down by a descendant of the original Hugo Baskerville in 1742 who warned his sons "to forbear from crossing the moor in those dark hours when the powers of evil are exalted."

Upon hearing the legend in its entirety, Holmes declares it to be a fairy tale. He is more interested in hearing the details surrounding Sir Charles Baskerville's death. Footprints of a huge hound were found near Baskerville, but there were no marks on his body. Baskerville had a weak heart, and apparently died of fright at the sight of the hound. Shortly before his friend's death, Dr. Mortimer had caught a glimpse of a great black beast that gave Sir Charles Baskerville a terrible fright.

Always the rational man, Holmes puts aside a supernatural explanation and begins collecting facts, rather than legend, to account for Baskerville's death. Before they actually leave Baker Street, there's an interesting exchange between Watson and Holmes. Holmes suggests the gloomy moor surrounding Baskerville Hall certainly seems like an appropriate place for the devil to work his evil. A surprised Watson says, "Then you are yourself inclining to the supernatural explanation?"

"The devil's agents may be flesh and blood, may they not?" replies Sherlock Holmes. With that he sets his plan in motion. He sends Watson to Baskerville Hall to guard Sir Henry Baskerville and make written reports on anything that happens there. Then, while pretending to stay in London, Holmes travels to the moor and hides in a hut where he can watch for the ghostly hound—and for flesh-and-blood agents.

Strange sounds are heard on the moor. Ghostly howlings echo in the night and chill the souls of those who hear, especially Watson, who says, "There rose suddenly out of the vast gloom of the moor that strange cry which I had already heard upon the borders of the great Grimpen Mire. It came with the wind through the silence of the night, a long, deep mutter, then a rising howl, and then the sad moan in which it died away. Again and again it sounded, the whole air throbbing with it, strident, wild, and menacing."

Soon another death occurs.

An escaped convict is running for his life across the moor, pursued by the hellishly howling beast. He falls over a cliff and dies, his body smashed on a rocky ledge below. Once again the crazed hound has claimed a victim—again without even touching the body.

But now Sherlock Holmes is hot on the trail as the murderer's scheme unravels. Holmes uncovers the true identity of Mr. Stapleton, a naturalist living on the moor, who is actually another descendant of Sir Charles Baskerville. Stapleton plans on inheriting the Baskerville estate as soon as his hellhound kills Sir Henry Baskerville.

For the hound that scared the older Sir Charles Baskerville to death belongs to Mr. Stapleton (whose real name is Rodger Baskerville). Part hound, part mastiff, it is a huge strong beast Stapleton bought in London and brought out to the moor to make the Baskervilles think that the legend was true and the hound was coming after them. He painted the poor beast's jaws with a smear of phosphorus so that its snarling teeth would be surrounded by a ghastly glow as it bounded over the darkened moors.

Late at night, Holmes and Watson send Henry Baskerville into the treacherous, bog-filled moor, hoping to lure the Hound out. They encounter the hound just as it jumps at Henry. Watson describes it as it emerges from the darkness. "My mind [was] paralyzed by the dreadful shape which had sprung out upon us from the shadows of the fog. A hound it was, an enormous coal-black hound, but not such a hound as mortal eyes have ever seen. Fire burst from its open mouth, its eyes glowed with a smouldering glare. . . ."

Running before it, his face filled with horror, is Henry Baskerville. The huge hound leaps in the air and is about to rip at Henry's throat when Holmes and Watson fire their revolvers at the beast.

It falls dead on the moor. And the legend dies with it. Stapleton, who tried to murder his way into the fortune, vanishes on the moor, falling into one of the endless bogs and never emerging.

The Hound of the Baskervilles had its origins in a legend Arthur Conan Doyle heard from B. Fletcher Robinson, a journalist and veteran of the Boer War who gave Doyle a tour of the moors near his home, where the legend was strongest. Though there was no real curse of the Baskervilles, there really was a Baskerville family. They were friends of Robinson, who borrowed the name from them.

In a preface to the novel Doyle acknowledged the source of

the legend by writing, "This story owes its inception to my friend, Mr. Fletcher Robinson, who has helped me both in the general plot and in the local details. —A.C.D."

A more general inspiration for the novel can be found in legends from all across Europe featuring monstrous black dogs who appeared in the forms of wolves, werewolves, or packs of wild dogs. The howling of a wild hound on the moors was said to foreshadow impending death, and it's easy to see how such an eerie sound might lend itself to a supernatural explanation. This echoes the superstitions of the Middle Ages, when people believed that the devil or a demon often appeared in the form of a huge black dog or, as it was known, a hellhound.

Doyle tapped into these legends and made it appear that the Hound of the Baskervilles was demonic in origin because of the hellish glowing colors around its mouth and eyes. And though this was later explained to be the result of phosphorescent paint, the eerie howling still sends a shiver up the spine.

Fletcher Robinson was also at the center of another real-life curse, one which might be called the Mummy of the Baskervilles.

In a March 16, 1959, newspaper article called "The Mystery of Baskerville," journalist Peter Evans interviewed Harry Baskerville, who told him about Robinson's death soon after he "started a fateful investigation into an Egyptian mummy's curse."

Doyle had considered Robinson's sudden and mysterious death the result of the curse. The article quoted Doyle as saying, "I warned him against concerning himself with the mummy. I told him he was tempting fate by pursuing his inquiries. . . ."

Supernatural Tales

Many modern readers are familiar with Arthur Conan Doyle's Sherlock Holmes stories, but he also wrote many stories dealing with the supernatural. Like his adventure and historical novels, they are not very well known today, although they may hold a key to his character.

Doyle had an intense interest in supernatural subjects, both in fiction and in real life. In fact, one of his short novels, *The Parasite,* mirrored events in his own life.

Published in 1884, *The Parasite* shows what happens to a skeptical scientist named Professor Austin Gilroy when he comes face to face with the supernatural. In the beginning of the novel Gilroy considers supernatural subjects such as séances and mesmerism (hypnotism) to be hoaxes. As a young and popular biology teacher he thinks hard sciences are the only subjects worth studying. But his colleague Professor Wilson has a different idea. Wilson teaches psychology, but he's also studying psychics and mesmerists from all across the world in order to "dig the foundations for a science of the future. . . ." According to Gilroy, Wilson is wasting his time studying nothing but maniacs and charlatans.

Despite their vastly different beliefs, Gilroy likes Wilson and accepts his invitation to a party where a woman from the West Indies is scheduled to demonstrate her amazing psychic powers. He plans on being a polite but skeptical observer and attends the party expecting to see one more charlatan at work. But then the psychic, Miss Penclosa, demonstrates her hypnotic control over one of the guests at the party—who happens to be Professor

Gilroy's fiancée, Agatha. When she falls into a trance, Gilroy is convinced there might be something to it. But for the final proof, he volunteers himself as a subject for Miss Penclosa. He, too, falls into a hypnotic trance and from then on returns time after time to see how powerful she really is.

Soon Gilroy falls totally under her spell. Day by day he grows pale and weak—while she grows strong and vibrant. Gradually he realizes she's like a psychic vampire who takes control over his soul and feeds on it, draining him of his willpower. He also sees that she's trying to make him fall in love with her and ruin his engagement to Agatha.

Gilroy finally manages to break away from Miss Penclosa by locking himself into his room so that he can't go to her anymore. She grows weaker when he stops visiting her. But although she can no longer drain his psychic energy, she can still control him from afar. With this telepathic power she causes him to fall into trances and make a fool of himself by spouting wild theories in his lecture class. He also commits a robbery while under her control and attacks one of his colleagues, beating him so badly that the man almost turns him over to the police.

Finally Gilroy snaps out of a trance—just as he's about to throw acid on his fiancée's face. He returns to his senses just in time to stop from hurting her. Dazed, he looks at the clock and sees that it is three-thirty in the afternoon. Later on he finds out that the psychic died at exactly three-thirty—ending her life and her control over him at the same time.

The Parasite reflects Doyle's belief in telepathy, hypnotism, and other psychic powers. Strangely enough, the events in the novel mirrored later events in Arthur Conan Doyle's own life.

Initially he was a very rational and skeptical man, but he found himself drawn to the world of spiritualism and began to attend séances where mediums would supposedly contact the spirits of people who had died, who would then talk to the living through the medium.

As a member of the Society for Psychical Research, Doyle attended séances all across Europe and the United States and praised many of the mediums for their amazing powers. He also believed in spirit photography, in which faces of the departed appeared in otherwise normal-looking photographs.

The skeptical man of science had become convinced in the supernatural even though many of the mediums he believed in were proven to be frauds. In fact, Doyle became good friends with one of the men responsible for uncovering "supernatural" hoaxes—the great magician Harry Houdini.

In the years after World War I, while Arthur Conan Doyle was visiting mediums whom he believed helped him communicate with those who'd passed on—particularly his first wife and his son, who had died from war injuries—the great magician Harry Houdini was exposing many of these mediums as frauds.

If anyone had the qualifications, it was Houdini. When he first started out as a magician he performed the same tricks in a carnival act that mediums around the world were passing off as supernatural acts.

Houdini was also a master of special effects. After starring in a film called *The Master of Mystery* as a hero who performed several amazing escape tricks, Houdini jumped into the world of films. He served as a special-effects man to create illusions on screen and he also produced several of his own films. This knowledge of special effects and fakery showed him how many of the so-called mediums were performing their tricks.

One famous hoax that had deceived Arthur Conan Doyle was a photograph on which dancing fairies allegedly appeared. Like many other people familiar with photographic effects, Houdini showed that this and other "spirit photographs" were actually nothing more than double exposures—one image printed on top of an already existing image. In the case of the dancing fairies, they were shown to be illustrations cut out from an advertisement and double-exposed with another photograph.

Houdini also demonstrated how most of the world-famous mediums often used props and accomplices to levitate tables in the dark, ring buzzers or bells during séances, and summon spirits from the other world, who often turned out to be nothing more than cloth with phosphorescent paint, much like the demonic dog from *The Hound of the Baskervilles.*

Aside from duplicating many tricks mediums performed, Houdini also caught them in the act by turning on lights while they were using props to make sounds or summon "ghosts." He often had police detectives attend séances with him so that they could charge the mediums as frauds.

Despite the fact that they were on opposite sides, Houdini and Doyle became good friends and often visited each other while on tour. Houdini also attended a séance in which Doyle and his wife were convinced Houdini's mother had sent him a message from beyond. But Houdini wasn't convinced. For one thing, his mother didn't speak English—in which the message was delivered—nor did her alleged spirit mention anything significant enough to convince Houdini it was a genuine communication.

The two men went their separate ways, Doyle praising the psychic powers of many mediums even after they admitted they were frauds, and Houdini launching a crusade to protect the public from the hoaxers. Inevitably this caused a falling-out between the two men, as each of them crusaded for what they believed in.

Though many people believe Houdini came out the winner in their arguments over the matter of spiritualism, in a way Doyle was the one who proved that the dead could come back to life.

In his short story "The Final Problem," Arthur Conan Doyle killed off Sherlock Holmes by having him and his greatest enemy, Professor Moriarty, tumble to their deaths over Reichenbach Falls. Doyle had tired of Holmes and wanted nothing more to do with him.

But his reading public raised a fuss and demanded more stories about the great detective. Holmes was so popular that Doyle had no choice but to grant him a reprieve and bring him back from the dead for several more adventures.

Chapter

6

Phantoms
of the Opera

Gaston Leroux

The Man Behind the Monster

A boat ripples silently in an underground river, docking against the rough concrete shore with an echoing thump. Then a skeletal figure in mask and cloak steps out. The figure has come to play a concert beneath the Paris opera house, a ghostly concert that few will ever hear.

The figure is the Phantom of the Opera, one of the most frightening and fascinating characters ever created by a horror writer. The man who created him was Gaston Leroux, a world-famous French newspaper reporter who began writing novels when he faced a real-life horror of his own—he was running out of money.

Gaston Leroux was a large man with a large appetite for life. Photographs of him show a bearded and dark-suited barrel-chested man who could easily plow through the waves of people he met on four different continents.

He wrote about war and revolution and natural disasters for his Paris newspaper, *Le Matin,* which sent him wherever danger could be found. His on-the-spot newspaper stories made him a famous and respected writer who was always expected to be where the action was, whether it was Europe, Africa, Asia, or even Antarctica. Leroux became one of the first globe-trotting reporters, and in his travels he faced more danger than many of the characters he would later write about.

By the time he was in his late 30s, he was tired of the newspaper business—just as he had tired of his earlier career as a lawyer. Leroux was the kind of person who, if he no longer enjoyed his work, simply stopped doing it. And as far as lawyers went, he would have been happy if all the lawyers in Paris also quit at the same time he did. In Leroux's opinion, the lawyers he worked with made justice impossible rather than probable.

After he grew tired of writing about the troubles of the world, he embarked on a career as a novelist—so people could read his books to escape from their troubles.

Naturally, Gaston Leroux did things his own way. Since mysteries were very popular at the time, especially the adventures of Sherlock Holmes written by Arthur Conan Doyle, Leroux decided it would be a good idea if he wrote a mystery novel—but not the usual kind. In his novel *The Mystery of the Yellow Room* (1909), he wrote a story where the killer turns out to be the detective investigating the murder. And the real hero of the novel just happens to be a globe-trotting reporter . . . much like Gaston Leroux.

The reading public loved *The Mystery of the Yellow Room.* This novel and a sequel, *The Perfume of the Lady in Black,* made Gaston Leroux one of the most well known mystery writers in the world. But his most famous novel was yet to come.

In 1909 he published a book that is still a best-seller today. In fact, several movies and musicals and operas have been based on that book in recent years.

The book was *The Phantom of the Opera,* and in it Leroux created a monster that his readers not only feared, but felt sorry for at the same time. For the Phantom of the Opera was a human monster whose horrifying looks condemned him to a lonely life in the caverns beneath Paris, where he played his sad, stirring music.

The Monster Behind the Curtain

The Phantom is first seen—or rather, not seen—backstage at the Paris opera house when two young ballet dancers named Jammes and Giri come running into the dressing room of La Sorelli, one of the leading ladies of the opera. They tell her about the ghost they've seen, or at least they think they've seen, because the phantom never appears long enough for people to be sure what has passed before their eyes. All is dark again after they see a flutter of his coat or a glimpse of his face.

But what a face it is. The skin is drawn so tightly over his face that he looks like a skeleton. His eyes are dark and set so far back that they can hardly be seen.

The rest of his body is also like a skeleton, but he wears a fancy dress suit, like a man on the town or an undertaker. And this is how he attends the opera.

The Phantom has his own private box seat in the highest tier of the opera. No one else is ever allowed in there. The managers reserve the box for him. They never see him enter or exit the box, but they hear him move about inside and they hear his deep, rich voice. But whenever they look inside the box, they see nothing.

And whenever the stage crew tries to find the Phantom, he vanishes before their very eyes. He does this by dropping through trapdoors, sliding behind curtains, crawling through secret passageways and tunnels, and passing through wall-length mirrors that are really revolving doors. To keep from being discovered, he descends into the cellars of the Paris opera house, down through

five levels of subbasements that are full of costumes and stage props.

He goes down through these cellars until he is deep in the earth, where the cellars connect with the catacombs, mysterious tunnels dug into the stone 2,000 years ago.

And then he climbs into a boat on the shore of a dark, still lake and rows out to a house in the middle of the water.

This is the hidden home of the Phantom of the Opera.

But why does he haunt the opera house? That is the question Gaston Leroux answers in his novel.

The phantom is a musician of genius who has been working on an opera for 20 years. It is an opera of such beauty that it casts a spell on anyone who hears it. It is an opera that could have been written by an angel. A sad angel.

For the Phantom is in love with a beautiful young singer at the opera. Her name is Christine, a girl with golden hair and blue eyes. Though she is beautiful, no one thinks she will ever be a great opera star because, unlike the other great singers, she has never had a professional music teacher.

Or so the world thinks.

Christine does have a teacher. He is an unseen teacher whose voice comes to her in the darkness. A voice from the walls, from the ceilings, a voice that teaches her the beauty of music.

At first she thinks the voice belongs to the Angel of Music her father told her about when she was a young girl. All great musicians were supposed to receive a visit from the Angel of Music at least once in their lives—when they were the saddest or when they were thinking of giving up. And then, unexpected, would come the angel, whose voice had such divine harmony they would remember it all their lives and capture just a bit of it in their own music. And whenever they thought of the visit, they would hear that music deep inside their hearts.

Christine always thought that one day the angel would come to her. And the Phantom lets her think he is the angel. His voice is as unearthly and beautiful as the face is hideous. With the power of his music and his voice, he enchants her, finally appearing to her with his frightening face hidden behind a mask.

With his help, she masters her voice. One night when the star of the opera cannot sing, Christine takes her place. As soon as she opens her mouth, the crowd of thousands falls silent, hypnotized by her sweet, heavenly voice. Nothing like it has ever been heard before by any audience in the Paris Opera.

It is as though they, too, are hearing the voice of an angel.

But the Phantom is not an angel. He has constructed a maze that traps people who search for him and eventually causes their deaths. It is also believed that he's the one who caused a 12,000-pound chandelier to crash onto the audience.

When Christine falls in love with another man, a handsome young aristocrat named Raoul, the Phantom kidnaps Christine and imprisons her far below the theater. Unless she agrees to marry him, he will destroy the theater and everyone in it, using barrels of gunpowder that have been left behind by French troops who once were stationed in the huge opera house.

The Phantom almost carries out his threat. But Christine wins her freedom at the last minute, when she lifts the Phantom's mask and gazes at his real face. Instead of shrinking back in horror, she kisses him on the forehead. And that kiss breaks a "spell" that has hung over the Phantom for so many years. Until now he has been separated from humanity, a monster who dwelt in the shadows. Christine's acceptance frees him from that prison of his tormented mind—and he suddenly acts human for the first time.

He frees Christine and Raoul, who has also been kidnapped.

He frees a secret policeman who has also been captured.

And then he vanishes from Christine's life, just as easily as he vanished in the secret tunnels of the opera.

The Catacombs of Paris

There really is a secret city beneath the French capital. It has tunnels instead of streets. And there is an underground lake.

This subterranean world is known as the Catacombs. For more than 2,000 years a maze of tunnels has been dug deep beneath Paris, carving out limestone blocks to be used in building the great houses and palaces in the French capital.

Since Paris is known as the City of Light, perhaps this underground stone quarry should be known as the City of Dark. There are almost 200 miles of catacombs beneath the city. Over the centuries they have been used as cemeteries, places to hold Christian masses, hideouts for criminals, bunkers for soldiers, caves for explorers . . . and a home for the Phantom of the Opera.

Just as he used the real Paris opera house for aboveground scenes in the novel, Gaston Leroux also used the Catacombs for his underworld scenes.

And in the novel he brought together creatures from two different worlds, a beauty and a beast, through the one thing they had in common—the love of music.

The Opera of the Phantom

Gaston Leroux was obviously familiar with the opera. During his era it was a great form of entertainment. The stages were huge, with room for hundreds of actors. The costumes were elaborate and the sets were built at great expense, using famous artists and craftsmen to create an artificial world for the singers and the actors to perform in.

Unlike modern entertainment on television that makes the world seem small, the goal of opera was to make the world seem large and the actors larger than life.

Leroux had spent his early days as a critic for a newspaper called *Echo de Paris*. It was his job to review plays and operas for the paper. And so it is quite easy to imagine Gaston Leroux, the bearded writer, haunting the operas and theaters of Paris night after night.

This familiarity with opera is evident in scenes where the Phantom acts like a critic, constantly writing letters to the managers of the opera house, telling them what operas to perform, what singers were bad, and what singers he wants to hear more of. Reading these whining notes from the ghostly critic is like being let in on a private joke of the author, who is making fun of the way he used to write about operas himself.

But what of the greatest opera in the world, the opera written by the Phantom in the novel? It was called *Don Juan Triumphant*.

The first time Christine heard the soft cry of the violin, she followed the sound to a secret passageway. The music was so beautiful that she felt it commanded her to find the source. And the source was the Phantom, who spent his life creating an opera of such beauty that it would turn him beautiful in the eyes of anyone who heard it.

And with the music came his voice, loud and strong enough to fill a cathedral, singing deeply, "Who so believes in me shall never die!"

The Phantom was a true artist who could create beauty from great sorrow. When Christine tried to describe the sound of *Don Juan Triumphant* to Raoul, she said it "seemed to me at first one long, awful, magnificent sob. But, little by little, it expressed every emotion, every suffering of which mankind is capable. It intoxicated me; and I opened the door that separated us."

And there in the depths of the opera house, she found the Phantom of the Opera performing his haunting music.

The idea of that magical opera never died. *The Phantom of the Opera* struck a chord with the reading public, a chord that is still echoing more than 80 years after Gaston Leroux wrote his great novel.

And today the strains of the Phantom's opera, *Don Juan*

Triumphant, can be heard in Andrew Lloyd Webber's recorded version of *The Phantom of the Opera,* music of the night that sounds as magical as if it were written by the Phantom himself.

Chapter 7

Martians, Morlocks, and Invisible Men

The Martians Are Coming—Again

When the Martians landed in Grovers Mill, New Jersey, on the night of October 30, 1938, British author H. G. Wells was not surprised. After all, his 1898 novel *The War of the Worlds* had predicted just such an invasion of cylindrical ships with strange-looking creatures slithering from out of their metal shells to blast away at humans with their heat rays.

But that was fiction.

This invasion was fact. Or so it seemed to the six million listeners of NBC radio's "Mercury Theater of the Air," a popular radio show hosted by Orson Welles. The famous young actor went on the air at 8:00 that night, and by the end of the hour people were running in the streets, looking for Martians. Phone lines were jammed as people tried to warn one another, and in some cities the streets were crowded with cars full of people eager to drive away from the invaders.

The following morning the *New York Times* reported that the broadcast had caused a panic around the country. A later report on the broadcast estimated that nearly one million people believed the Martians had really landed.

Of course, what really happened was that Orson Welles and his writing and acting troupe had updated the famous H. G. Wells novel *The War of the Worlds* and set their radio play in modern-day America instead of in Wells's turn-of-the-century England.

One reason the show was so successful was the manner in

which it was presented. In the beginning of the show an orchestra was playing music from the Meridian Ballroom in New York City. The music was interrupted by a series of news bulletins from various locations where Martians had supposedly landed. Since radio was a major source of information for the public, when realistic "bulletins" about invading Martians interrupted the music, many listeners naturally thought it was happening for real—making this one of the most talked-about radio shows in the history of broadcasting.

Another reason the show was so successful was the imagination of H. G. Wells, whose novel was a sensation when it was published in 1898. And its basic theme was still an attention-grabber 40 years later.

H. G. Wells, a man with a prophetic sense of the promises and perils that science offered to humanity, had already written *The Time Machine* and *The Invisible Man,* which were also destined to be classics. But it was *The War of the Worlds* that made him one of the most famous writers in the world—and perhaps beyond.

Wells was in his early 30s when *The War of the Worlds* was published. By that time he had toned down his tendency to lecture his readers—stemming from his brief stint as a teacher with a special interest in science—and was more interested in giving his readers an adventure story from start to finish. Along the way he presents a thought-provoking look at humanity when its world is turned upside down. In the novel much of England is destroyed, and London is left in smoking ruins. The social habits of the population are also destroyed as they run panic-stricken from the invaders, often turning against one another because of

H. G. Wells

the fear and hunger consuming them.

In this compelling adventure story, Wells also presented an accurate glimpse of the future. The Martian weaponry he described in 1898 is very close to present-day "Star Wars" technology.

"It is still a matter of wonder how the Martians are able to slay men so swiftly and so silently. . . . This intense heat they project in a parallel beam against any object they choose, by means of a polished parabolic mirror of unknown composition, much as the parabolic projector of a lighthouse projects a beam of light." It almost seems that Wells was writing a blueprint for today's advanced laser technology, which bounces laser beams off mirrors and satellites for communications or weapon systems.

Along with the frightening weaponry was the utter strangeness of the Martian creatures wielding it.

The first Martian landing is thought to be a meteorite crashing into the earth in a rural part of England, its impact blasting a deep pit. But soon the meteorite is discovered to be a huge, cylindrical metal ship, 30 yards in diameter. While onlookers stare in shock, part of the cylinder starts to unscrew. And then a Martian starts to emerge.

Two luminous eyes appear from the dark shadows of the ship. "Then something resembling a little grey snake, about the thickness of a walking stick, coiled up out of the writhing middle, and wriggled in the air towards me—and then another."

More and more tentacles appear, and a big, grayish, slithering thing about the size of a bear climbs out of the ship, glistening like wet leather. As the first creature falls into the pit, another hideous creature begins climbing out.

The invasion begins. Puffs of smoke cloud the pit as brilliant flashes of flame strike the villagers who have gathered around it, their bodies glowing and then falling to the ground, charred and unrecognizable.

More ships land and more terrible weaponry faces humanity as giant machines emerge from the ships. "Machine it was, with a ringing metallic pace, and long, flexible, glittering tentacles (one of which gripped a young pine tree) swinging and rattling about its strange body." Mounted on huge tripods higher than a house, these machines stalk and stomp through the landscape.

The Martians use poisonous black smoke as well as heat rays to destroy everything in their path. The army is helpless against them, their massive artillery having no effect on the invaders. In fact, as we learn throughout the horrifying novel, nothing can stop the Martians—except the earth itself.

One by one the Martians suddenly begin to fall and die off. They are killed not by any great invention, but by small invisible bacteria. Previously unexposed to our atmosphere, the Martians are vulnerable to the very germs that humanity has long been immune to. As the last invader dies in putrefying agony, the War of the Worlds comes to an end with a shudder instead of a bang.

In an epilogue to the novel the narrator wonders if the Martians will invade again. After all, they may be able to learn from their mistakes and plan another invasion. Will humanity be ready for them the next time?

Either way, something good may come out of the tragic invasion. For the narrator poses yet another question. If the Martians can travel to other planets, then what can prevent humanity from developing the necessary technology for space travel? To the narrator and to Wells himself the answer was obvious—as indicated by the title of one of his later novels, *The First Men in the Moon.*

From Science to Fiction

Herbert George Wells was a teacher and, for a short period of time, a drama critic for the *Pall Mall Gazette.* But one of his life-long interests was science and its effects on society. Coupled with this interest in science was a broad knowledge of history, as he demonstrated in one of his major nonfiction works, *The Outline of History.*

Wells combined his interests in science and history to create a future history that ultimately became his first novel, *The Time Machine.* An earlier version of the novel was a series of essays about a hypothetical trip into the future. These essays had a preachy quality about the wonders of science and read like lessons to an uninformed reader. Fortunately, an editor who'd taken an interest in Wells's earlier work convinced him to give the idea another chance—this time as a real novel with characters more interesting than the machinery Wells was so interested in.

This gave him a chance to explore the issues he'd been concerned with ever since he was a young boy. In a 1906 collection of essays called *The Future of America,* H. G. Wells wrote, "I remember that to me in my boyhood speculation about the Future was a monstrous joke. Like most people of my generation, I was launched into life with millennial assumptions." Belief that the world was due to end soon had been around since the beginning of time. As a child Wells had a vague impression that it might happen in his lifetime or shortly afterward. "There would be trumpets and shoutings and celestial phenomenon, a battle of Armageddon, and the Judgment."

With this background, it's little wonder that in his fiction Wells often cast a wary eye on the future.

In *The Time Machine,* Wells takes us on a journey 800,000 years into the future, as seen by a scientist who is referred to throughout the novel only as The Time Traveller.

The narrator of the story regularly attends the weekly gathering of psychologists, journalists, and doctors at the scientist's house, where the Time Traveller regularly startles them with ideas they find hard to believe. But the narrator knows him better than the others and realizes there may be something to his strange stories.

At one gathering the scientist's talk of time travel is met with laughter and skepticism. But at the next meeting he demonstrates a small model of his machine. This model is "a glittering metallic framework, scarcely larger than a small clock, and very delicately made. There was ivory in it, and some transparent crystalline substance." The scientist displays the machine on a table surrounded by candlelight. After explaining that one lever pushes it into the future and one sends it into the past, the scientist turns it on.

"There was a breath of wind, and the lamp flame jumped. One of the candles on the mantel was blown out, and the little machine suddenly swung round, became indistinct, was seen as a ghost for a second perhaps, as an eddy of faintly glittering brass and ivory; and it was gone—vanished!" After demonstrating the model, the scientist tells them about a larger machine he's built so that *he* can travel into the future.

"Parts were of nickel, parts of ivory, parts had certainly been filed or sawn out of rock crystal." This version isn't quite finished yet, but the scientist tells them he's going to test it on himself very soon. "Upon that machine . . . I intend to explore time."

The Time Traveller does exactly that and returns from the future just in time for the next regular meeting. Starved for meat—perhaps because he hasn't eaten anything but fruit in ages—he has a hearty meal, then slowly tells the story of his travels, beginning with the strange workings of the machine as he increased its speed through time.

"Night followed day like the flapping of a black wing . . . I saw the sun hopping swiftly across the sky, leaping it every minute, and every minute marking a day." Since he's only moving in time, not in space, his machine stays in exactly the same spot, but his surroundings change rapidly. "I saw trees growing and changing like puffs of vapour, now brown, now green; they grew, spread, shivered, and passed away."

When the Time Traveller finally stops his machine he is surrounded by a group of small, gentle people known as Eloi, who are apparently happy and none too smart. They are easily tired and their attention wanders. In a way they are a lamblike race of humans. They take him to a huge gray building where there is plenty of food—fruits only, however, since in this future the people are all vegetarians.

At first the Time Traveller sees this world as a paradise. The land is rich and lushly green, fed by silver-ribboned rivers. But gradually he finds that the people of the future are in effect lambs waiting for the slaughter. For their peaceful paradise becomes frightening during the long nights. That's when the dominant group of this future world, and underground race known as Morlocks, emerge from huge round wells burrowed deep into the earth. From the wells comes a steady sound, "a thud-thud-thud, like the beating of some big engine."

From this nightmarish underworld the Morlocks come up into the great halls where the peaceful Eloi sleep—and gather up the unfortunate ones they bring back to their subterranean lair for food.

The Time Traveller gets his first glimpse of the Morlocks in the hours before dawn.

> *The moon was setting, and the dying moonlight and the pallor of dawn were mingled in a ghastly half-light. The bushes were inky black, the ground a somber grey, the sky colourless and cheerless. And up the hill I thought I could see ghosts. There several times, as I scanned the slope, I saw white figures. Twice I fancied I saw a solitary white, ape-like creature running rather quickly up the hill, and once near the ruins I saw a leash of them carrying some dark body.*

Later the Time Traveller discovers that the Morlocks are the ones who have taken away his Time Machine and hidden it inside the bronze pedestal of a white marble sphinx. In his effort

to regain the Time Machine, he finds out more about the Morlocks. The strange ghostlike creatures only come to the surface of
the planet at night. From living underground so long, their skin
has turned white and sluglike, giving them their eerie appearance.

The Morlocks run the great machines that thud-thud-thud
underground. They're the ones who provide the Eloi with clothes
and other necessities. They're the ones who keep them happy—
much like cattle ranchers keep their herds.

The Time Traveller realizes that the Eloi and the Morlocks
have their origins from the same race. But he's traveled so far into
the future, 800,000 years, that a typical Morlock looks like something from another race entirely. "It was a dull white, and had
strange large greyish-red eyes . . . flaxen hair on its head and
down its back." It appears to run on all fours, or just holds its
forearms very low. Although the Morlocks appear to be apelike
in nature, they are the cleverer of the two races.

The Time Traveller theorizes that the Eloi were originally the
aristocracy in a utopialike society. The Morlocks were their ser-
vants, who ran the machines and performed all of the necessary
work. The longer they lived underground, the more they changed
from the Eloi. Their skin became whitish from living underground. Their eyes glowed. Sunlight hurt them, restricting them
to moving about on the surface only at night.

Since the Eloi had no challenges to face in everyday life, they
became weak and dull-minded. They no longer had to learn how
to survive—the Morlocks did that for them. Though they still
look basically human, they're as passive as a flock of sheep—leaving the Time Traveller to fight the Morlocks on his own.

He journeys into one of the underground lairs of the Morlocks and barely escapes with his life. Using some matches to frighten them away, he manages to escape. Finally he enters the chamber where the Morlocks have his Time Machine. While they scramble all around him, nearly overwhelming him, he starts the machine and escapes into the past. He returns to his home in London, tells his story, then takes off once again. And the rest is history. An unknown history, at that—because the Time Traveller never returns.

The Invisible Man

While many critics didn't see much to like in *The Invisible Man* and considered it minor compared to *The Time Machine* or *The War of the Worlds,* the novel has its fair share of chills. This time around there are no monstrous predators descending upon humanity. Here the monster is a man named Griffin who, like many of Wells's characters, is a scientist.

But Griffin is not a likable man. He steals from his father so that he can continue with his experiments, resulting in his father's death—since the money wasn't his father's to begin with, his father ends up shooting himself.

Griffin manages to concoct drugs that first decolorize the blood, then the rest of the body, experimenting on a cat before trying it on himself. The cat turns misty, then invisible, until finally "there remained two little ghosts of her eyes." When he tries the process on himself, Griffin goes through a painful trans-formation.

It happens slowly. First his face turns like white stone. Then he undergoes "a night of racking anguish, sickness and fainting. I set my teeth, though my skin was presently afire, all my body afire; but I lay there like grim death." Finally the pain passes and he begins to fade. "My hands had become as clouded glass. . . . My limbs became glassy, the bones and arteries faded. . . . At last only the dead tips of my fingernails remained, pallid and white, and the brown stain of some acid upon my fingers."

Griffin is now the Invisible Man. Unfortunately he is also mad. Or madder than before. He steals without a second thought and assaults anyone who crosses his path. After all, as the Invisible Man he can get away with anything.

When a man named Kemp, whom he considers a friend, turns him in to the authorities, the Invisible Man escapes and then warns the world that from now on he's the man in charge. "The game is only beginning," he writes in a letter to Kemp.

> *This announces the first day of the Terror. . . . This is day one of year one of the new epoch,—the Epoch of the Invisible Man. I am Invisible Man the First. To begin with the rule will be easy. The first day there will be one execution for the sake of example,—a man named Kemp. Death starts for him today. He may lock himself away, hide himself away, get guards about him, put on armour if he likes; Death, the unseen Death, is coming.*

Griffin is right. Death is coming—for him. When he attacks Kemp, several men try to stop him. A brawl and a chase scene follow, with the Invisible Man alternately chasing or being chased. As he catches Kemp for the final time, one of the men hits the Invisible Man with a spade, and the rest of the men join in the fight until he stops fighting back. And then Griffin's face shows once more. But now it is the face of a dead man. Killed in the struggle, his body slowly regains its form and color.

The Invisible Man's short reign is over.

H. G. Wells wrote many other novels and stories of fantasy and science fiction, but today he is remembered mostly for *The War of the Worlds, The Time Machine,* and *The Invisible Man.* In much of his fiction Wells showed a remarkable gift for prediction. Many of the things he wrote about came to pass, such as lasers, atom bombs, and space travel. Fortunately earth hasn't been invaded by Mars. Yet. But if such an invasion ever comes, perhaps another one of his predictions will come true—and earthlings can avoid another War of the Worlds by hopping into one of his time machines made of parts of nickel and ivory and rock crystal.

For Further Reading

* * *

Mary Shelley

Frankenstein. New York: Bantam, 1984.

The Journals of Mary Shelley. New York: Oxford University Press, 1987.

The Last Man. Lincoln, NE: University of Nebraska Press, 1965.

* * *

Washington Irving

Diedrich Knickerbocker's A History of New York. Tarrytown, NY: Sleepy Hollow, 1981.

Ghostly Tales of Washington Irving. Pierrmont, NY: Riverrun, 1990.

The Legend of Sleepy Hollow. New York: Morrow Jr. Books, 1990.

Rip Van Winkle. New York: Morrow Jr. Books, 1987.

* * *

Robert Louis Stevenson

Black Arrow. New York: Dell, 1990.

The Body Snatchers and Other Stories. New York: NAL-Dutton, 1988.

A Child's Garden of Verses. New York: Simon and Schuster, 1984.

Dr. Jekyll and Mr. Hyde. New York: NAL-Dutton, 1987.

Island Landfalls: Reflections from the South Seas. North Pomfret, VT: Trafalgar Square, 1988.

Kidnapped. New York: Puffin, 1983.

Treasure Island. New York: Scholastic, 1988.

* * *

* * *

Bram Stoker
Dracula. New York: Bantam, 1983.
Lair of the White Worm. New York: Zebra, 1979.

* * *

Sir Arthur Conan Doyle
Adventures of Sherlock Homes. New York: Macmillan, 1985.
The Hound of the Baskervilles. New York: Viking Penguin, 1981.
The Memoirs of Sherlock Holmes. New York: Ballantine, 1985.
The Return of Sherlock Homes. New York: Viking Penguin, 1987.
The Sign of Four. New York: Ballantine, 1987.
The White Company. New York: Morrow Jr. Books, 1988.

* * *

Gaston Leroux
The Mystery of the Yellow Room. Cutchogue, NY: Buccaneer Books, 1975.
The Perfume of the Lady in Black. Cutchogue, NY: Buccaneer Books, 1975.
The Phantom of the Opera. New York: NAL-Dutton, 1987.
The Secret of the Night. Cutchogue, NY: Buccaneer Books, 1975.

* * *

H.G. Wells
The Complete Short Stories. New York: St. Martin's, 1988.
The Invisible Man. New York: Bantam, 1987.
The Island of Dr. Moreau. New York: NAL-Dutton, 1977.
Selected Short Stories. New York: Viking Penguin, 1990.
The Time Machine. New York: Bantam, 1984.
The War of the Worlds. New York: Bantam, 1988.

* * *

Index